Zahara's Quest

The Rise of the Light, Volume 6

H. M. Gooden

Published by H. M. Gooden, 2019.

This is a work of fiction. Similarities to real people, places, or events are entirely coincidental.

ZAHARA'S QUEST

First edition. November 13, 2019.

Copyright © 2019 H. M. Gooden.

ISBN: 978-1989156162

Written by H. M. Gooden.

Also by H. M. Gooden

The Dragons of the North
Mai's First Date

The Raven and the Witch Hunter
The Raven and the Witch Hunter: The Spirit of Big Bear
The Raven and the Witch Hunter: The Wedding
The Raven and The Witch Hunter: Honeymoon and Full
Moon Blues
Wendigo

The Rise of the Light
Fiona's Gift
Dream of Darkness
The Stone Dragon
The Phoenix and the Witch
Dragons are Forever
The Raven and the Witch Hunter
Zahara's Quest

Standalone

Watch for more at https://www.hmgoodenauthor.com/.

Table of Contents

To my besties, my yars.

I can still remember the red sands of Wadi Rum and the Pillars of Wisdom.

Whenever I close my eyes and think of Petra, we are standing there together.

Life may have separated us, but you are always in my heart.

CHAPTER 1

Z ahara looked down the alley, alert to the possibility of observation. So far, the only movement she sensed was that of dried leaves, swirling in eddies, in the corner between the buildings where she was sheltered.

It wasn't the most inspiring sight, but it did allow her the necessary privacy to change to a more comfortable form without anyone seeing her. Allowing the relaxing tingle of warmth to spread over her skin, Zahara sighed deeply.

There, that's better.

When she opened her eyes and looked down, she was grateful to see the familiar tawny fur she loved. Now safe in her preferred shape, she took off without hesitation from the alley into the adjacent woods, leaving her mundane day job far behind.

The distance between work and home wasn't far and Zahara preferred to travel in her four-legged fox form whenever possible. It was liberating to shed her human skin at the end of the day, and the side benefit of avoiding traffic wasn't a downside either. She felt more at home as a fox in general, but it also found it was a great way to relieve stress at the end of the day. She loved running as fast as she could, and it always took her away from the daily hassles working for a busy travel company in Edinburgh could create.

She arrived at her apartment less than twenty minutes later, changing back in the small forested area which bordered her street. She didn't worry too much about being seen here. Her area was quiet, but after years of learning to make sure she wasn't inadvertently seen by anyone, her habits were firmly engrained. She'd had the luxury of growing up surrounded by others who could also transform into creatures of the earth but knew how ordinary humans reacted to anything 'other'. She got more than enough practice being different as a woman of South Asian descent in Scotland and was certain she didn't need any more discriminatory crap in her life.

Zahara brushed her clothes off with a contented sigh. The weather had held off raining and her clothes had made the transition intact for a change. With Edinburgh weather, it wasn't uncommon for them to end up soggy and/or dirty. For once, the grey December clouds had remained benign.

Moving smoothly to the front door and unlocking it, she scanned the room automatically after switching the light on. Her place was a small, but cozy, basement suite of a three-story brick house. She'd been lucky to get such a good deal on a one bedroom so close to her work and nature, but she was fairly certain it was due to family connections. With her practical nature, she'd chosen to accept the help and leapt at the chance to leave home.

Her parents had been less than thrilled she'd wanted to move in the first place, so giving them peace of mind by living in a place owned by family friends was the least she could do. It also made them feel like they could supervise from a distance, which she grudgingly accepted as the way things were going to be until she got married.

Moving into the bedroom, Zahara kicked off the clothes she'd worn at work, throwing them haphazardly in the vicinity of the laundry basket as she grabbed her pajamas from the night before and slipped back into the cozy flannel. She hit the kettle to switch it on to boil, even though her mum would frown if she could see her. It was faster to make instant chai, even if it wasn't nearly as good.

As if she'd summoned her by her thoughts, Zahara's phone, discarded by the door on her way in, began to ring.

"Hello, Mum?" said Zahara after she saw the number was, indeed, from her parents. *I wonder why she's calling so early.* She spoke to her parents several times during the week, but never before eight or nine. Her concern increased when she heard a quick inhale and sniff as if her mum was fighting back tears.

"Zahara?"

The sound of her mum's voice, tremulous and weak and far from her normal rich and happy tones, caused a pit to form in Zahara's stomach.

"Mum? What is it? Is Dad okay? My brothers?"

A wet laugh followed, but it was brief and not at all reassuring.

"Yes, dear. Everyone is fine. I just...got some news. I need you to come home tonight. Can you make it?"

Zahara looked at the clock before checking the calendar on her wall and winced. Her boss was pretty accommodating, but it was only Wednesday and they were right in the middle of a busy week leading up to the holidays.

"I'll talk to Mira, but I'm sure she'll say it's okay if I tell her why. What happened?"

Zahara wasn't sure she wanted to know. She'd never heard her mum like this before. She instinctively knew that whatever she was wanted home for was something big. It was good to know it didn't involve something to do with her immediate family, yet something was clearly very wrong. The last time she remembered hearing her this upset was when one of her distant relatives in Pakistan died.

"I...can't tell you over the phone. Just tell Mira we have a family emergency. Come home, Zahara. Please. It's important."

Zahara disconnected the call after reassuring her mum she'd be there as soon as possible and placed it on the counter. She was strangely numb with worry and the possibilities of what could be wrong that were racing through her head weren't helping. After everything she'd seen in the past few years, she had a strong suspicion whatever her mum wanted to talk about wouldn't be something she wanted to hear.

She absently scratched her shoulder through the fuzzy pajama top and looked at it regretfully.

Damn.

Sighing as all her plans for a relaxing evening with a good book dried up and blew away, she went back to her room to pack a small bag she could carry on her back as a fox and changed back into her jeans.

The trip to her parents took a little over an hour by road and a little more than that traveling on four legs. The extra time wasn't terribly inconvenient though, as it allowed her to avoid all the evening traffic by taking the grassier, more direct route, which was far more pleasant. Two hours later, she arrived at the Khan family farm.

It was tucked off the highway down a gravel road and from the front it appeared to be a quintessential Scottish cottage, cozy yellow, with a small duck pond in front and trees sheltering the cheery yellow door from the gloomy grey of the rain.

But the truth was even more magical.

Behind the house was the Khan's direct access to the magic of Summerland. Because they were all powerful earth mages, they'd had a connection to the local god of the earth as far back as she knew.

At one point in time, Robin had helped her ancestors out and ever since, her family considered him a close friend and mentor. Zahara didn't know all the details, just that she'd never known a time without him. He was basically an uncle, albeit a slightly crazy, very distant, and scary-powerful uncle who frequently acted in a socially inappropriate fashion.

Drawing her attention away from the comforting familiarity of her childhood home, she transformed into her human form and walked up the stairs. After she turned the doorknob, she entered more hesitantly than normal.

"Hello? Anyone home? Mum? Dad? Guys?"

The first sign something was horribly wrong was the lack of the permeating aroma of food. Usually at this time of day, there would be something either on the counter or recently put away and the deliciousness would still be lingering in the air.

Her mum had a thing about making sure everyone had food at any given moment, so this was a shock in and of itself. No one was in the kitchen, but a small voice answered from the living room.

"Zahara? We're in here." Her dad called out from the living room, sounding the same as always.

Some of the knot which had lodged in her chest at the suppressed tears she'd heard through the phone released. Putting her bag down by the door, she removed her shoes and headed to the living room.

The sight greeting her was one of deep mourning. All three of her brothers were there. They sat on the two couches across from each other, looking solemn and worse, silent. Usually it was impossible for them to go more than a few minutes without teasing each other or fighting.

Her dad stood next to her mum's chair with his hand on her shoulder. She had her hand up to grasp his and had laid her head on it as if she was exhausted. When Zahara entered, she looked up and gave her a weak smile.

Zahara went over and gave her mum a hug, feeling her squeeze back tightly for a few beats longer than usual before holding her out to look at her, smiling through puffy eyes. There were new lines on her mum's face and she realized as she looked between the two of them her parents were aging. Although they still had mostly dark hair and skin that shone with the sun's blessing, several new white hairs peaked out from the black like white-tailed deer hiding on farmland.

Was something wrong with one of them?

Stricken, Zahara hardly noticed the way her mum glanced at her sons, then locked gazes with her dad during the long pause before she spoke again.

"Thanks for coming so quickly, *jaani*. It's good to have you home. I received some troubling news today."

Zahara waited impatiently. She hated it when anyone drew things out like this, let alone her mum, who was so open you usually had to remind her not to over-share.

"I had a phone call today. Do you remember your cousin Seema?" She paused, waiting for confirmation from Zahara before continuing. "She told me your great aunt Reema has...passed."

Zahara watched as her mum broke down into tears. Her dad looked down helplessly, patting her head with one hand. Unable to stop herself, Zahara knelt at her mum's feet.

"I'm so sorry, Mum. Were you very close?"

Zahara watched with confusion when she shook her head vigorously.

"No, I've never met her. That isn't the problem." She stopped speaking again and seemed to be fighting for the right words. "She was the keeper."

"The keeper? What do you mean 'keeper'?"

She'd never heard of Reema or a keeper, but the reaction told her both were important. She waited as her mum took several deep breaths and composed herself.

"She was the guardian of our family. It is because of her we have been at peace from other creatures for so long. She inherited the protectorate, which has kept us safe from the jinn who would have destroyed us centuries ago. A powerful foe who has continued to search for us with the goal of ending our family line since ancient times."

Although this was something Zahara had never heard before, the words filled her with a weird sense of knowing, almost like she was being reminded of something she already knew, deep down. But how? She'd never heard of her family having a guardian or keeper that she could recall, and certainly nothing about a jinn who wanted to destroy them.

"So what does that mean?" A horrible thought crossed her mind. "Are you saying we're in danger? Is that why you're so upset?"

Her mum looked at her with dark brown eyes full of anguish and nodded slowly. "Yes, that's exactly what I'm saying. With Reema's death, the spell cast to protect us is broken. None of us are safe. This particular enemy is known to be relentless and full of a hatred matched only by his enormous power. We cannot right any wrong or make any amends, as the affront he vowed to revenge himself on is that of our very existence. He is a purist and I am certain time has not changed that. I was told he believes we are unnatural and defective as we are a mixed race of part human, part jinn. If he has his way, he would wipe out our entire family and end us forever."

Her last words were barely a whisper, and once she shared the news, she fell silent. Zahara looked around the room wildly, taking in the solemn, silent faces of her brothers and her father as she attempted to process the enormity of what she'd just heard. They didn't appear nearly as surprised as she was and she suspected her parents had already filled them in while waiting for her to arrive.

As she considered what she'd heard, her horror grew. Somewhere out there was a powerful being set on the annihilation of her entire family? It sounded crazy and yet...

Zahara slumped from her kneeling position to sit abruptly on the floor as her mind went blank. She felt completely unable to process anything.

She'd faced evil and prejudice before, but something about this particular combination was completely overwhelming. It was so personal, yet not. She'd never heard of this jinn but he wanted to kill her entire family just on principle?

It was so bizarrely evil.

Her mind slowly picked up speed. The cleansing burn of anger filled her chest, and she stood up as her natural stubbornness took over from fear, her eyes flashing a dark topaz. She looked at her parents and lifted her chin.

"So, what can we do?" She turned to her brothers, who merely shrugged. When she set her jaw two looked away before her brother, Amir, finally answered.

"I can't do anything right now. I wish I could. I'm right in the middle of my last semester. Exams are coming up. If I take off now, I'll fail. I can't afford any time off if I want to get into med school next year."

"Same for me. I can't get away until at least May, after finals," Suf added.

Mo tilted his head helplessly in agreement, gesturing at his brothers to show he was in the same situation.

Zahara grunted an acknowledgment. Her brothers weren't trying to flake out, even if part of her secretly felt they were. Someone needed to finish school to support the family. While they all had a fair amount of earth magic, that didn't and couldn't pay the bills in the normal human world. One of her brothers had been accepted to the University of Edinburgh for law school and another had gotten into Cambridge, but none of that mattered if they didn't pass their undergraduate degrees.

She knew she was the only one free to do anything right now. While she did have a job, her boss was an old family friend and very forgiving about the kind of situations that had a tendency to come up when you weren't entirely human. It was through her she'd met her best friends when they'd come to Scotland in the first place a few years ago. Sometimes, she couldn't help being frustrated at the way her life seemed to be controlled by people who knew her, but at times like this, it was helpful rather than annoying.

She knew she'd have a job to come back to if she needed time off. When she'd called Mira to let her know she had a family emergency, instead of being upset or saying no, Mira had told her to take as much time as she needed.

As it turned out, she may need to take her up on the offer.

"What can I do? If they can't help right now." Zahara flicked a glance at her row of brothers, the same familiar irritation at the unfairness simmering inside her.

She'd always chafed at the restrictions society placed on her in her various forms but had never had a chance to do anything to right the wrongs that seemed so obvious. Maybe this was her chance and she could somehow use this to her advantage.

She thought back to when she'd first met her friends, remembering how Cat had taken on the white, preppy wanker at the petrol station when he'd felt entitled enough to tell Zahara to go back to her own country. Cat had sure changed his mind in a hurry. Even now, she couldn't help smirking at the memory. Maybe this was her chance to change someone else's mind, permanently.

Failing that, she was always happy to kick some butt.

Her dad gave her a proud smile. "I had a feeling you would say that, which is why we called you home. You needed to be aware of the danger so you could protect yourself, but I told your mum you would be able to fix this. I said, 'our Zahara has an ability to solve problems like few others I know.' I am certain you will put this jinn in his place."

Zahara blinked as his expression became dark and vengeful. His normally bushy and au natural eyebrows drew together ominously, giving him a stern look she rarely saw. He usually encouraged them to turn the other cheek and pray for others to have their hearts and minds changed for the better. To take the high road.

It was a surprise to hear him say he thought she could fix this, but even more shocking to see him look so angry.

"Really? How?"

He let go of her mum's hand and took hers instead, looking at her seriously as he placed his other one on her cheek. "Of all of my children, you have the brightest fire, *jaani*. You may be the smallest, but you are my scrapper, the fighter of the crowd. I am proud of all of my children, and your brothers are becoming wonderful men, but you have the rare strength of character I believe will be required to fight an injustice over a millennium old. You've never settled for the status quo before, and your contrary streak is what is needed to save our family now."

She shook her head. "But I still don't understand. What injustice do I have to settle? And why now?"

Her dad looked at the clock on the wall and held up a hand. "It is late. We all need to go to sleep. Conserve your energy. We will discuss this more tomorrow when your mum and I have had a chance to think on it further. It was important to have you all home tonight, to let you know what is coming and to comfort our hearts, but we do not have to set things right all at once."

He stepped back, patting her hand as he returned to her mum's side. "Sleep. We'll talk in the morning, I promise. Hopefully, the sun will bring some clarity with it."

Zahara searched their faces for answers, but both were closed. She knew when they were done speaking and her mum sealed it when she stood and kissed her cheek. "It's good to have you home, *jaani*. It's been a long day. I'm tired now but we will discuss this more tomorrow. Over some real chai, okay?"

Zahara blushed. Somehow, even in the middle of such devastating news, her mum managed to throw in a teasing jibe about her lazy tea making. "That sounds good, Mum. Good night. I'll see you in the morning."

She watched her parents walk out of the room to their bedroom, her dad keeping his arm around her smaller mum as she leaned on him. They looked frail all of a sudden. Where had her powerful dad and vibrant mum disappeared to in the last few days?

"They are ridiculously cute together, aren't they?" Amir came to stand beside Zahara, bumping her arm to catch her attention.

"Yes, they are. I won't settle for anything less than that." She squinted at him warningly, taking in his neat goatee, perfect eyebrows, and preppie collared shirt, and lightened the mood. "You'd better not, either."

He laughed. "Don't worry, little sis. I have no plans to getting tied down anytime soon. I'm still waiting on someone special and they haven't come into my life yet. Besides, school takes all my energy right now. What about you? Anyone special in your world I need to have a talk with?"

She punched him lightly on the arm. "None of your business. Like I'd tell you so you could interrogate them? I think not."

He gave her a cheeky grin before gesturing to her other brothers. "Well, you don't need to worry about me. But you may need to worry about these two. As you know, they aren't safe to be out in public at all."

"Hey!"

Mo and Suf protested from the couch, and Zahara felt some of her anger and anxiousness fade away as the everyday teasing between her brothers brought her back to normal.

"I love you guys."

CHAPTER 2

Zahara stretched out in bed, looking around her old bedroom. She was always more comfortable here than in the city but had left to make her way when she'd graduated at eighteen. True, she could have stayed home indefinitely, and culturally, it was still appropriate for an unmarried woman to remain at home with their parents until marriage. But that path hadn't been for her.

She'd felt a need to find her own way in the world and had been just stubborn enough to strike out to find it. She blamed at least part of her firm-mindedness on growing up with three older brothers, but had only been on her own a short time when Robin had enlisted her to help with Cat and Evelyn's school exchange trip.

It had turned out to be the best time of her life and had taken her desire to be the captain of her own destiny further than she could have ever imagined from when she'd lived at home and dreamed of freedom. Not only had she made lifelong friends, she'd discovered a side of her personality she liked a lot.

For the first time in her life, her smaller size hadn't held her back. With her friends, she was part of a group of five equally fierce women. And nothing accelerated forming friendships faster than using elemental powers to defeating opponents who meant to plunge the world into darkness. In the process, Zahara had discovered she was completely capable of taking down opponents using just her magic and her wits.

Remembering the odd conversation from the night before, she got out of bed, dressed in some of the old clothes she'd left in her room to wear whenever she visited, and headed to the kitchen.

Hopefully Mum is awake.

While she was happy with her independence, nothing beat coming home to her mum's cooking. True, she could cook for herself, but something about her mum doing it for her was not only comforting but tasted better most of the time as well.

She let her nose guide her as the familiar scent of chai simmering on the stove wafted down the hallway, making her feel a little like old commercials of the toucan following the smell of Fruit Loops through the jungle.

Pulling up a chair at the breakfast nook, she watched her mum bustle around, pulling items out of the fridge and generally creating magic in the kitchen. Sometimes, she wondered if it actually *was* magic. Her mum could create miracles in this room but maybe that was a normal mum trick. Either way, Zahara loved eating whatever her mum cooked.

"Good morning."

Her mum looked over, giving a tired smile when she saw Zahara perched on the chair. "Good morning, *jaani*. I hope you slept better than I did. I couldn't stop thinking about poor Reema."

"Did you get more news? I thought you said you'd never met her." Zahara's eyes widened. "How did she die, anyway?"

The corner of her mum's lip quirked up at Zahara's sudden barrage of questions. "As far as I know she died of natural causes—no one said any differently. I didn't know her personally, as she wasn't around when I visited my cousins. But she was very well-known in the family and others spoke of her often and fondly. I think I never had a chance to meet her because we live here. I regret it now. I missed out on knowing a wonderful woman, which makes me very sad. In a way, she was kind of like Robin. Mysterious and magical."

Zahara nodded. It was the way she felt about some of her heroes from childhood. Women who'd stood up for equality in times when women had less freedoms than now. "You said we could speak more about what I need to do today to protect the family?"

Gratefully, she accepted the steaming cup of chai her mum placed in front of her, blowing on the creamy, fragrant tea while she waited for an answer. Sighing, her mum pulled up a chair and placed her own cup down.

"Yes, I did. Your dad and I discussed it after we went to bed and we believe you'll need to go back to deal with it."

"Back? Do you mean to Pakistan?"

She shook her head. "Yes, and no. Our extended family lives in Pakistan now, but we didn't originally come from there."

"What?"

Zahara was floored. All she'd ever heard from her parents was about their heritage in Pakistan. How they'd immigrated to Great Britain for a better life and left family behind who couldn't or didn't want to move away. She'd visited a few times since childhood, but her home and heart were a hundred percent in Scotland. Hearing there was another piece of her past was a complete shock.

"Before Pakistan, there was Jordan."

Her mum sipped her tea delicately, watching Zahara's reaction as she processed the sudden revelation.

"How come I've never heard about this before?"

Her mum raised a shoulder, giving a slightly guilty smile. "It was so long ago. I never lived there, nor did your father, and it never seemed important before. However, now that things have changed, well, at this point it might be crucial."

"But how? If none of our family has lived there for a very long time, why would I need to go there?"

Her mum gave her a patient smile. "Reema is from Jordan and my cousins said she returned there before she passed. I don't know how old she was when she moved to Pakistan, just that she did before your father or I were born. I get the impression she was quite old. Either way, from that point on our family grew and flourished there. But, our story began long before that."

Zahara thought for a moment, looking out through the kitchen window at the sun streaming through the trees before she spoke slowly, trying to work it out in her head. "So I need to start where the legend began?"

She nodded. "Yes. I wish I knew more, but according to my cousins, Reema was always very secretive. I'm told she didn't spend much time around others, even her loved ones."

Her mum abruptly got up and opened one of the cupboard doors, pulling out a plain brown envelope before shutting the door and coming to sit down beside her again. She placed the envelope on the counter, sliding it in front of Zahara then waited expectantly for her to take it.

Reaching down, Zahara placed a cautious hand on the plain package. "What's this?"

Her mum angled her chin toward the envelope. "I don't know. I was waiting for you to open it."

Mystified, Zahara slowly opened the flap and turned the envelope upside down. Something heavy and cold fell out into her hand. As it uncoiled, she realized she was holding a breathtakingly beautiful necklace. Turning it over, she whistled soundlessly at the sight of the large, dark green emerald glowing quietly from the center of an orange-gold setting.

Wide-eyed, she looked at her mum. "I don't understand. What is this?"

She shrugged, tilting her head. "Other than the obvious, I don't know. It came in the mail yesterday, just before I received the phone call. I didn't open it because it had your name on it. One thing I am sure of is that the necklace and the news of her passing are connected. I believe Reema herself wanted you to have this. I think, although I have no way to know for sure, you need to take it with you when you go."

"What?" Zahara heard her voice squeak with surprise and cleared her throat.

Her mum nodded. "Look at the address."

Zahara turned the envelope around, seeing her parent's address on the front, but her name as the addressee. She narrowed her eyes. "How did she know who I was?"

Once again, her mum shrugged. "I have no idea. But this is why we called you home. Not only to tell you about the passing of someone you don't know but because of this package. Of all of our children, you may be the only one with a flexible schedule right now, but there is more to this duty being placed on your shoulders. For whatever reason, this is your quest. I do not believe it was ever something your brothers were meant to do."

Zahara sat back in her chair. It was overwhelming; the idea that somehow, this had been predetermined. She remembered her friend Cat complaining more than once about feeling she had no control over what happened to her, that she was a mere pawn in a larger game. She then thought of her friend Mai's reaction when she'd found out she and her husband, Jake, were part of a prophecy involving their children.

For the first time, she thought she understood how they felt.

It was as if she was being swept along a raging river. Without any energy or direction from her, she was being carried downstream by the events occurring around her. She gazed down at the emerald and knew without question this mysterious necklace would be a touchstone for whatever was coming. As she turned it over and over in her hands, feeling the smooth but ornately carved surfaces of the innocent looking, beautiful necklace, she felt with all her heart it was the key.

But the key to what?

Putting the necklace down, she inspected the empty envelope. Maybe it held a clue of some sort, something that could point her in the right direction.

A piece of paper fluttered out.

"Wait, what's this?"

When she'd dumped the necklace out she hadn't noticed it there, distracted by the far more obvious bling that had fallen out of the envelope. As she unfolded it though, she realized the letter was every bit as valuable.

Written in Arabic in the spidery hand of someone either very old or whose hand had been shaking with emotion, it proved challenging to read.

MY DEAREST LITTLE ONE. You must be very confused right now, for which I am sorry. I had hoped never to draw you into this battle, but alas, my strength is failing. I must beseech you to finish my work and defeat our mutual enemy.

You must bring the necklace to the place of all knowledge, where your journey will begin. Do not come alone. You will need assistance from others to complete the trip.

I cannot guarantee your success, for which I am most sorrowful. Please know I believe you can do anything you set your mind to. You have hidden depths that will help you. You must not fail, because If you do, so too will the family tree wither and die.

Be safe, be wise, and most of all, be yourself.

Come quickly, and be careful.

Love,

Reema

ZAHARA ALLOWED THE paper to float down to the table. For the first time in her life, she was grateful for the boring Arabic/Quran reading classes her mum had forced on her in childhood. Even so, it had been a painful read.

The strangest thing of all was how the letter had been directed to her, as if she was an old friend or confidant. It didn't make any sense. She looked at her mum. "How does Reema know me?"

Her mum raised her hands, palms up. "She obviously felt she did, but not from your father or I. As I said before, I've never met her myself."

Zahara shook her head, trying to clear the cobwebs away. When that didn't work, she stood, taking one more sip of the sweet chai before placing it down again and drew her shoulders back.

"It appears I have a new mission. Reema wanted me to take the amulet back, but not alone. She says in the letter I will need assistance." Zahara looked accusingly at her mum, still suspicious she wasn't divulging all she knew. "How come you never mentioned anything to me before now? And why does Reema's death cause us to be unprotected?"

Her mum sighed, gesturing for Zahara to sit again. "It wasn't an intentional omission, I promise. This story is so old I never even thought about it. I don't know all the details, only what I've heard from others in passing."

She looked at her pleadingly when Zahara didn't move.

"Please sit, *jaani*. I will tell you everything I know about our origins, but I'm sure much has been kept from me as well. We left Pakistan when I was just a child and as so often happens, some family legends may have been left behind as well. Not out of malice, but simply because they were no longer needed or deemed important."

Zahara sat, doing her best to suppress an impatient sigh. "Please continue. I'll try to be open-minded."

She received a warm smile as her mum patted her hand. "That's my girl. Your fire will take you a long way, but patience will get you to the goal. Never forget you need both to succeed in the world."

Zahara nodded, but her mum's words struck a chord. She knew impatience sometimes got the best of her, but if she truly needed to save the family, she'd have to work harder on it.

"I'll do my best. Please, tell me everything you know."

Her mum took a sip of chai before folding her hands in front of her as she began to tell the tale.

"Once upon a time, our family lived in the desert. They made their home on the shifting sands and were simple, happy folk. Everything changed when one day, your ancestor fell in love with a powerful magician in the court of Suleyman the Magnificent. She was a simple girl and expected nothing, but somehow, this powerful mage fell in love with her in return. They shared a deep love, but one which was forbidden."

Zahara was intrigued already. A forbidden love? She secretly dreamed of such a thing sometimes, although she'd never admit it for fear her brothers would tease her mercilessly. She tuned back in.

"They were not meant to be together for one simple reason. You see, not only was he a powerful jinn. Even more dangerously, he had already been promised to wed another, the daughter of a jinn even more powerful than he when she came of age."

Zahara's mum paused for another sip of her tea so she used the opportunity to comment.

"So then what happened? I can't imagine that worked out well."

She knew full well how important arranged marriages could be, even in modern times. Breaking that sort of promise today often led to huge issues, and she could only imagine that hundreds of years ago, it would have been enough to cause a family's downfall, up to and including death.

Her mum smiled sadly. "No, it didn't work out well. When the other jinn found out, he flew into a rage at the dishonor which had been shown to him, vowing to kill the jinn and everyone he loved."

The beginning of unease trickled down Zahara's back as she realized what was coming next. *Shades of Romeo and Juliet, except with magic?*

"Your ancestor fled with the protection of her jinn lover, and for a time, they were safe and happy together, hidden away from the world. They had a son and were content with their small family. But somehow, the angry jinn found where they were hiding and came to destroy them as he'd promised. Fearing the worst, our jinn ancestor protected his love and his son, but at great personal cost. He was said to have been destroyed in the battle which ensued, but not before his love found a spell to protect our family, hidden in the books brought with them from Suleyman's court. She managed to save her son, and the spell has continued to protect us from the jinn until the present day."

"But with Reema's death, something changed." Zahara nodded as the pieces clicked into place.

Her mum nodded. "Yes. I believe the spell has, or is, failing. Perhaps it is because Reema kept it intact until now, although I do not know why or how."

Zahara considered the story her mum had shared. It filled in some of the blanks about the evil chasing them now but left her full of more questions than answers.

"If the spell lasted so long, why did it fail now? Suleyman lived, like, six hundred years ago. Why would Reema be the only one who could keep it going?"

"I don't know," her mum replied, lifting her hands helplessly. "All I know is that for some reason, my only daughter has been given the task of saving us all. As a mother, I can't help worry about this situation on many levels."

She regarded her mother's pinched eyebrows and tight mouth with sympathy. She knew how much she worried about her mum, dad, and brothers, but she didn't have children. Even from speaking with Mai, she'd seen how her friend's focus had changed the minute she'd had her babies. She could only imagine how worried her mum was.

"I'm sure if it's meant to be, it will be. I'll be fine, Mum." She broke into a smile. "Listen to me! Now I'm the one sounding all platitudey-Judy, like Robin at his irritating best. Clearly, things are going to work out. In the letter, Reema mentioned I needed assistance. But Amir, Suf, and Mo are too busy to come. I wonder who she meant."

"You are right; this is not their quest. Take some time to think on what it could mean. I'm sure something will come to you."

Zahara nodded and sipped her tea. *Maybe if I called my girls? No, they're all busy. I don't want to add to their stress load right now.*

Mai was married and super busy with the triplets. Cat was in university and probably on a similar schedule as Zahara's brothers. Vanessa was newly in love and working on a hit new TV show. As much as Zahara enjoyed her antics, she didn't want to interrupt a happy time after what she knew had been a miserable year for her. Evelyn was around somewhere, but probably too busy protecting the world to help with a small mission like saving Zahara's family.

Zahara drank the last of her chai, looking at the bottom of the mug with disappointment. "Thanks, Mum. I'm sure you're right."

CHAPTER 3

Zahara spent the remainder of the day the way she normally did at her parents' house. After eating as much as she could, she hung out with her brothers in front of the TV and chatted about their respective weeks until they were slightly less bloated, then headed out to the backyard where their Summerland gate was.

As they'd done since childhood, they each shifted into their unique earth forms to practice their abilities together. Each sibling took on the form of a different earthbound animal. Amir was a coyote, Suf a cougar, and Mo a gazelle. Zahara was the smallest of the four, but not one of her brothers would ever hint at her being slower or weaker. Not these days at least.

Growing up, they'd played tag in the way that only siblings with earth magic can, with the added twist of playing predator and prey, and they knew better than to taunt her from years of her coming out on top when they least expected it.

Mo technically should have been prey given his gazelle form, but because he was larger than the others it was generally a fair fight. Zahara was tiny as a fennec fox and in real life, she would have been at the mercy of a real cougar or coyote. But in this family, she was a fierce competitor.

Today, they were playing a version of capture the flag. They had divided into teams of two and the winners were the team who stole the other team's flag and got it to the gate first. As so often was the case, Zahara and Amir teamed up and gave her other brothers a trouncing.

"Nice, sis. Glad to see you haven't lost your mad skills, what with living in the big city as a working girl and all," Amir teased, his nose wiggling as he smelled the air while waiting for their others to catch up.

Zahara tossed her head back, her large ears swiveling at the sound of panting as her other brothers approached. "Not too shabby yourself, bro. Nice to see all the studying isn't making you a fat and lazy hound dog."

"Ha!" Suf arrived in time to disagree with Zahara. "Says you. Have you seen his gut lately? I'm thinking he looks like an old, married uncle instead of a twenty-five-year-old man about town."

Zahara laughed as the two faced off against each other, coyote against cougar. While Suf was slightly bigger, Amir lived up to the cunning coyotes were known for. Just as she thought they were settling in for a good fight, they heard their mum calling.

"Later. I don't want to miss supper." Suf took off running, transforming as he did.

"Deal," said Amir. "Tomorrow, if we've got time. I'm going over to Al's to study tonight."

He transformed as well and they continued to snipe at each other in a friendly fashion the rest of the way to the house. Zahara hung back, admiring her brothers as they smacked each other randomly, or tried to trip each other. She had a strange sense of disorientation at the realization they were all in their twenties now. Still single, but maybe not for long.

Both Suf and Mo had serious girlfriends, although Amir hadn't been exaggerating when he said he was too busy. He was practically married to his school work, but she knew it meant he'd be an amazing doctor one day.

Suddenly, it struck her that if she failed to reset the spell, or whatever she was supposed to do, none of them would have any future at all. If there really was an evil jinn coming for her family, her brothers were at risk. It also meant she may never have nieces and nephews to play with, the way she and her brothers still played. Her will hardened.

Not on my watch. I'm not going to let that happen. Come what may, I will take care of this threat to my family.

Taking one last look over her shoulder as they sauntered home, Zahara wondered if Robin would make an appearance.

It'd be nice to have guidance from someone with a little more knowledge of these things.

THAT NIGHT, AFTER HER brothers had taken off and she'd said goodnight to her parents, Zahara climbed into bed in a more thoughtful frame of mind than the day before. After hearing about her ancestors and how the curse had come about because of a forbidden love, Zahara had no doubt she was meant to go on this quest.

But how could she accomplish her mission with nothing more than a necklace and a legend?

The only hard fact she had was the amulet with the emerald in it, which she was apparently supposed to take back to the place with all the knowledge.

What did that even mean?

She assumed it was back to the place her ancestors had originated from in Jordan, but where was that?

Rolling over in bed, Zahara lifted the necklace off her nightstand to examine it for the hundredth time. It didn't look like anything other than a pretty necklace with a large jewel. Hardly something mystical, or that looked able to beat an evil jinn bent on destroying her family. With a sigh, she put it down and turned the light off, snuggling under her covers as her eyes fluttered shut.

Her dreams that night were troubled. She wasn't particularly prone to prophetic dreams. Every now and then Robin would show up to tell her something, but generally she slept deeply and didn't remember what she dreamed about. This night was different. Her dreams were full of shifting sand and the hard, bone-chilling laughter of someone who meant her harm.

As she tossed and turned in bed, becoming increasingly more distressed, her dream lit up from within. A sense of calm descended and she looked around in confusion to see who was there, then smiled as the shape of a woman surrounded by light and a pair of translucent wings grew larger.

"Evelyn! What the heck are you doing here?" Zahara blurted as the figure of her friend became clear. When she heard how rude she sounded, she rushed to add, "Not that I'm not happy to see you, of course. But damn! I wasn't expecting to talk to you for a while."

Evelyn smiled, but her expression quickly became serious. "My dreams have been showing me things, dark things, that make me worry for you. But I can't quite see what's coming. It's like it's blurry, or hidden from me by someone."

Evelyn's brows furrowed and she looked briefly irritated before giving Zahara a sheepish look. "I'm accustomed to seeing what's coming more clearly, so this is a bit of a surprise and irritation. I actually came to see if you knew what was going on and make sure you were okay."

Zahara shrugged, letting her arms drop to her sides. "I'm fine right now, but I can't add much detail to your fuzzy dreams. All I know is some great aunt of mine from Jordan, not Pakistan, died and sent me an emerald amulet in the mail. I'm supposed to take the thing back to the 'place of all the knowledge' and defeat some evil jinn who's had a hate-on for my entire family for the last several hundred years or so."

Evelyn quirked an eyebrow. "Oh, you don't say? Well heck, child, if that's all, what are we so worried about? I guess I should just..." Evelyn paused. "Oh no, wait. Yep, that sounds pretty intense. Okay, in that case it's settled."

Zahara tilted her head. "What do you mean? What's settled?"

Evelyn tossed her head and gave her a mischievous smile. "Why, we'll be there tomorrow, of course. Make sure your mom has fresh pakoras ready. I'm hungry just thinking about the ones she made the last time we visited."

Zahara's mouth dropped open but before she could ask Evelyn what she meant by 'we', her alarm clock went off, ripping her out of the dream. She bolted upright in bed with her heart racing. She wasn't sure if it was from the nightmares she'd been having or from the surprise of hearing Evelyn say she was on her way, but either way, she was wide awake now.

She checked the clock, surprised to see it was already seven, and even more surprised she'd set her alarm in the first place. She had no memory of doing so the night before, but she'd been distracted. Maybe she'd set it out of habit. Either way, she was up and it sounded like she needed to get things ready for company.

Getting out of bed, Zahara dressed quickly and went to the kitchen. She needed caffeine, and she needed it now.

"Here, *jaani*. I had a feeling you'd be up early."

Gratefully, Zahara accepted the cup of coffee her father handed to her. Both of her parents were sitting at the kitchen table and if she wasn't mistaken, it looked like they'd been waiting for her.

"Thanks. What are you doing up so early? I'm not even sure what I'm doing awake yet."

She slumped into a chair at the table and took a deep breath of coffee scented air and sighed with pleasure. While it never tasted quite as good as it smelled, she liked what it did for her. Chai was tastier, but coffee was better for early mornings.

"Your mum spoke with your friend, Evelyn, the other day," her dad said, taking a sip from his own cup as he watched her.

"What? When?" Zahara jerked upright in her chair, almost spilling her coffee with the abrupt movement.

Her mum clucked her tongue. "Be careful. You don't want to burn yourself."

Zahara put the cup down on the table, carefully folding her hands next to it at the mild admonishment before looking at her mum. "Okay, tell me. When did you speak with Evelyn?"

Her mum smiled enigmatically then finally took pity on her. "She called me on the phone yesterday."

"What?" Of all the things Zahara expected to hear, this wasn't one of them.

A normal, mundane phone call to her mum?

"Yes, she wanted to make sure it wouldn't be too much of a bother if she came to visit. It slipped my mind with everything else that's been happening I guess. I'm sorry."

Zahara sat back in her chair. *So. Evelyn had already planned ahead of their conversation in the dream last night. Figures!*

"Huh. What else did she tell you?"

Her mum took a sip of her coffee before smiling again. "Not much. She gave her condolences and said she would be happy to join you on your travels. I must admit my joy at hearing from her during such a stressful time. Such a nice girl." Her mum glanced at her dad, adding, "and so powerful."

He nodded. "Yes, always nice to have powerful friends." He gave Zahara a stern look. "But don't think her presence means you don't have to be careful. Even with friends such as Evelyn, this jinn is dangerous and can do you incredible harm."

Zahara sighed. "I know, Dad. I've been thinking about it nonstop since I first saw the amulet. I vaguely know where I need to go, but I wish I had more information on what I'm supposed to do when I get there."

Her dad leaned over to pat her hand. "Have faith, *jaani*. We've never truly worried about you before. You may be the smallest of our children, but your spirit is mighty. You will overcome."

Zahara could feel his calm spread over her. Her dad was hands down the quietest one in the family, but when he believed in something, it was wholeheartedly and he was known to be unshakeable in those beliefs. It was nice to know he felt she was so capable, even when she wasn't sure he was right.

Zahara finished her coffee and excused herself. She had the overwhelming urge to go running and decided to head to the backyard alone. She shifted into her fox form between the patio and gazebo as she bounded across the boundary marking the doorway to Summerland.

Luckily, the passage was open this morning.

She felt the telltale shimmer as she entered into the other world Robin ruled as the uncontested king. The sun was high in the eternal summer sky, and dandelion fluff appeared to gently sway in the breeze. When she looked closer, she saw small glowing fairies, and with a canine playfulness, gave chase. Small yips of laughter escaped her as she scattered the nearest group high into the air then continued to race around in zig-zags for a while, clouds of white flying up in the air as she passed them.

The sudden sound of giggling caused her ears to prick up. Turning, she was in time to catch a small brown-haired boy dropping out of an old oak tree beside her.

"Robin! I've missed you!"

She gave him a lick on the knee before she caught herself. Sometimes, when she was in her animal form, her emotions spilled over before she caught them.

"Oops! Sorry! I meant no disrespect."

Zahara cringed at his feet, but he just laughed. The sound rippled over the peaceful glade like sunshine.

"Oh, my little kit! Do not worry. I am well pleased to see you, as well."

Zahara raised her head then cocked it sideways as she examined him.

"Robin, you look younger than the last time I saw you. Is everything well?"

He looked down at himself, lifting his arms to the side before slowly spinning around and finishing his twirl with a bow when he returned to center.

"Do you like it? I prefer to run around in this shape and form. Unless Evelyn is around, of course. She needs a man more than a boy." His eyes twinkled. "Don't give away my secret, but I'll always be a boy at heart."

Zahara shook her head as she chuckled. Robin would always be her lord and master, no matter what shape or age he appeared to her in. He was full of energy and fun, but she knew he and Evelyn had a more adult relationship than his current appearance would allow.

"Will you be seeing Evelyn soon? My mum told me she plans to come for a visit shortly, to help with our family curse."

Robin's face became serious. "Aye. I have heard. Do not worry about that. I am here to make sure you are ready for travel. Evelyn and Cat will arrive shortly to travel with you and provide aid when possible and required."

Zahara interrupted, her surprise overpowering her normal deference. "Cat? She's coming too? How come no one mentioned that?"

Robin brushed her question aside. "It is unimportant. I wanted to catch you now, before they arrived, to let you to know you will need my help this time."

While Zahara heard his words, she didn't like them. Robin always hinted around about helping them in the past if absolutely necessary but hadn't actually ever had to. The fact he was now telling her he'd actually *need* to this time made her stomach sink.

This was bad.

"What should I do, Robin? I have no idea how I'm supposed to achieve whatever is expected. All I know is I have to take a necklace somewhere in the Middle East. Can you give me a clue? Please?"

Zahara heard the plaintive sound of her voice and cringed. *God, I hate sounding like some weak movie princess.* She fancied herself more as the antithesis of that but her lack of direction was making her more confused than she liked.

Robin came closer to pat her head, stroking the fur gently. Zahara felt her concerns melt under the comforting tingle his touch left behind.

"Worry not, little one. As your parents have recently reminded you, you are more than capable of achieving your goal. It will be difficult, certainly, but you will have your friends. I will be there to help when needed. You must defeat the jinn permanently this time. There will be no other chance for your family to break the curse."

Zahara sighed, leaning against his leg for support. The task felt overwhelming. She only hoped she'd be up to the challenge.

CHAPTER 4

"So what exactly do you think you're doing with my man? Hmmm?"

Evelyn's familiar, sassy voice broke into Zahara's worry. When she opened her eyes, both Evelyn and Cat were standing beside them. She blinked. A moment earlier, no one else had been there.

Robin's hand dropped from her head and extended toward Evelyn as his smile lit up the glade. "My love! I was not expecting you quite so soon. It is marvelous to see you." His eyes crinkled as he turned toward Cat with an equally bright smile. "And you as well, of course, Lady Firebird."

Robin bounced away from Zahara to give Evelyn a peck on the cheek before resuming the childish, carefree dancing the girls were accustomed to seeing from him.

"It's nice to see you too, Robin," said Cat, greeting him more formally than Evelyn had before turning to Zahara with a squeal. "Zahara!" She held her arms out. "Can I give you a hug? I missed you so much!"

Zahara smiled, her tongue lolling out of her mouth as she jogged over to accept Cat's hug. She knew it was hard for Cat to resist patting her admittedly cute fox body, but Cat tried so hard to be respectful of her boundaries; she found it endearing instead of irritating the way it was when her brothers tried.

"Of course, Cat. How was your trip?"

Cat stroked her friend's head once before dropping her hand guiltily. "Nice and quick, as always. Evelyn found a gate in San Francisco some time back, so we didn't need to drive all the way to my parents' place. That was pretty convenient."

Evelyn and Robin were still saying hello, so Cat and Zahara kept their conversation and eyes to themselves. Shortly after Cat had come over to give her a hug, Zahara noticed Robin's form shimmer, becoming the attractive young man he appeared as whenever Evelyn was around. The other girls had learned to allow them some alone time whenever that happened.

When they finally rejoined them, Cat sighed with relief. "Okay, are we good now? Because I'm starving. Zahara, would it be rude to ask if your mom made food?" She wrinkled her nose, smiling with a hopeful look in her eyes.

Zahara shook her head, amused at her friend's barely concealed begging. "Come on! You've met my mum. Also, Evelyn called yesterday unbeknownst to me, so I'm sure she's got food ready as we speak. If you want, we can check out the kitchen situation first?"

Cat bobbed her head, looking thankful. "Yes, please!"

Robin smiled, including all three of them. "Give my best to Mr. and Mrs. Khan. I'll be in touch. Evelyn," he looked into her eyes, now speaking only to her. "I'll see *you* tonight."

Evelyn blew him a kiss and winked before turning to Cat and Zahara. "Let's go, girls. Time to figure out our game plan with the help of mom-snacks."

Laughing, the girls headed to the gazebo and walked through the shimmering curtain back through to the real world.

As expected, the moment they walked into the kitchen it was converted into a buffet. Mrs. Khan was overjoyed to have extra mouths to feed and hustled the girls over to the kitchen table.

"No, I don't need any help. Sit! Food will be out shortly."

"But I can..." Cat trailed off.

Mrs. Khan shushed her. "Sit. You three have much to discuss. I'll be back in a moment."

Cat looked helplessly at Zahara.

She shook her head. "Don't worry about it, Cat. Seriously. If she says she's good, she's good." Zahara smiled, leaning closer and dropping her voice. "Plus, she's worried about me right now and wants you guys to help keep me alive. You can bet she's going to go out of her way to make this amazing."

Evelyn leaned forward in her chair. "So what exactly is going on? I've been seeing some really disturbing things at night, but I'm having a hard time figuring out if they're real or not. It feels like there's a window between me and my dreams. I can't touch them or see what's happening as clearly as usual."

Zahara shrugged. "I can't tell you much. Right now, all I know is that an aunt, whom I've never met, recently died in Pakistan. An envelope with a necklace arrived in the mail addressed to me with a letter from her, saying I have to take it back to 'the place where the knowledge is kept'. Which apparently isn't in Pakistan. So I'm kind of stumped right now too. All I know is that it's imperative I do this. Oh, and apparently everything is tied to an evil jinn who hates my entire family tree. If I don't defeat him, we'll all die."

Cat whistled tunelessly. "Dude. That's pretty intense. So, where are we going?"

Zahara shrugged. "That's the problem. I don't know."

Evelyn interjected. "I may have an idea about where to start. Robin has a contact in Saudi we can gate over to. You mentioned earlier you're supposed to take the necklace somewhere other than Pakistan?"

Zahara nodded. "That's right. I just found out from my mum that while our immediate family came from there, prior to that we were from the Middle East. Jordan, to be exact. Our distant family member, the jinn the magic originally came from, was a court mage to Suleyman the Magnificent."

Cat nodded slowly. "That makes sense he would use beings with magic. I've been learning about him this semester in Middle Eastern history. He did some pretty impressive things, especially considering the time. I wonder how much of his 'magnificence' was because he had mages working for him. Something my textbooks have conveniently omitted to mention, of course."

Evelyn tilted her head in agreement. "Do you have any idea where his court was located?"

"He was a little bit everywhere. At the time of his rule, his empire was the largest in the world. He became the tenth Ottoman Sultan in 1520 and conquered Belgrade, Transylvania, Hungary, and all the way up to the Caucasus mountains. He ruled a long time and during his rule covered territory in Europe, Africa, and the Mediterranean. He died in 1566 and was buried in Constantinople, now called Istanbul."

"Hmm," Zahara said, feeling overwhelmed again. "That's a lot of territory to cover. But the most challenging part is it sounds like most of this happened after my ancestor left court."

"Well, it's a start. The court was located in Constantinople. Maybe if we headed that way? It's a direction and often thought of as a sort of the gateway to the Middle East," Cat suggested.

Zahara shook her head. "I don't know. For some reason it doesn't feel right. I highly doubt they would have tried to hide away somewhere so populated. Where's another place that would have been less settled but still considered a place of learning during that time period?"

The girls paused to think about locations while Mrs. Khan entered the room, carrying a large plate of food.

"There. Now eat up, girls. There's plenty here." Mrs. Khan winked as she brushed her hands off on her apron. "Also, I may have forgot to mention to the boys I was cooking for you, so you should have a few minutes alone before they smell it and descend. I recommend you move quickly."

Winking once more, she made to leave the room, but Cat stopped her.

"Mrs. Khan, I was hoping you could tell us more about where your family comes from. Zahara said she just found out they're originally from somewhere in Jordan. Do you have any idea where, exactly?"

Mrs. Khan sighed and turned around, pulling a chair out to sit at the table with the girls. She looked out the window with a thoughtful expression on her face.

"All I know is they travelled from the desert to Pakistan, which was a greener, easier place for them to use their magic. As I told Zahara earlier, I'd heard my parents mention a time when their ancestors had migrated from Jordan, but never any mention of a specific town or such."

Cat jumped in her chair. "That's it! I'm sure of it!"

Zahara turned to look at her, surprised at her forceful exclamation. "What is it?"

"Jordan!"

"I don't get it. We already know about Jordan." Evelyn shook her head. "What's so special about it?"

Cat leaned forward, waving her hands excitedly. "We all know Jordan is an ancient place. It was settled in caveman days and has been a place of relative stability in the Middle East for centuries. I'm wondering if it's possible your ancestors left Constantinople and fled to Petra."

"Petra?" Zahara echoed. "Why Petra?"

"Because Petra has been there for thousands of years. It's thought to have some kind of mystical significance to the local Bedouins. I'm wondering now if maybe some of the legends are due to the magic of those who settled there."

"I thought the hype was just in the *Indiana Jones* movies?" Evelyn raised an eyebrow.

Cat shook her head. "Nope. It's a real thing. Okay, maybe the Holy Grail isn't there, but what if Petra is where we need to go? It's probably one of the most important mystical sites in Jordan, if not the entire Middle East, and it's not as populated as other locations. If Jordan is where your family came from, we need to check out Petra."

Mrs. Khan replied, thoughtfully drawing out her words. "That's a good idea, Cat. While I'm not certain if you are right about my ancestors living there, it is known to be a special place in the desert. It has a protected water supply, which in and of itself would make it a good place for an earth mage to take up residence. The area is mostly desert now, but at one point it was said to have a large green oasis. Maybe your theory is correct."

Zahara shrugged. "Cat's the one with the history books, but I'm game to try. We can always head somewhere else if Petra doesn't pan out. How will we get there? Is Robin going to help with transport?"

"That's what he said. Saudi is right next door to Jordan, so his friend connection will work nicely." Evelyn took another helping of Aloo Gobi and considered the rice for a moment before shaking her head and bringing a fork to her mouth.

Zahara nodded. It did sound like things were lining up nicely, which was as reassuring as it was troubling. The letter had said she needed assistance and voila, Cat and Evelyn appeared. Robin had already weighed in, promising he'd help this time, which was as frightening as it was encouraging. And now Cat just happened to remember Petra was a mystical hot spot. Maybe her ancestor *had* gone there to hide.

It seemed like a whole bunch of coincidences were lining up, which conversely made Zahara believe they weren't coincidences at all.

"What do you think, Zahara?"

Cat was watching her with a worried expression and Zahara realized everyone had stopped talking and were waiting for her to say something. She forced her worry down for now. *Plenty of time to freak out later.*

Rubbing her neck, she smiled. "Sorry guys, I was just thinking about everything. We may as well head to Petra. I don't like not knowing or the fact we don't have any hard data on what we're getting ourselves into, but I'm not sure it can be helped.

I'm also more than a little uncomfortable with the way everything seems to be falling into place."

"What do you mean?" Evelyn asked.

Zahara pursed her lips. "Think about it. I mean, what are the odds you guys are both available to help? And Cat just happens to have information about the area we need to travel to from classes at school? Not to mention a mysterious emerald amulet necklace shows up in an envelope addressed to me the day after a long lost aunt I've never met dies. It sounds a bit more predetermined than I'm comfortable with."

"Ah. That." Cat leaned back in her chair, grimacing.

Zahara raised her eyebrows. "Yup. That."

Mrs. Khan stood up beside the table. Zahara had almost forgotten she was there until she moved.

Now, she took Zahara's hand and looked down with warm, brown eyes. "My darling *jaani*. Nothing in life is by chance only. We all have a greater purpose. This, my dear, is yours. You were born to be a fighter, a warrior for the light. We have done our best to raise you and your brothers to be good and honest people. Now, the family curse is upon us and will come to pass unless you stop it. It is your destiny. As much as I wish things were different, you are the one tasked with this quest. I can think of no one more capable."

Zahara looked into her mum's eyes. Seeing her conviction, she was reassured despite her fear. "I know you believe in me, Mum. I just wish I knew in advance how this would end. If I knew I'd be successful, maybe I wouldn't be so nervous about the journey."

Mrs. Khan smiled and squeezed Zahara's hand. "Half the fun of living is not knowing what the journey holds."

CHAPTER 5

Zahara checked her backpack for the tenth time. She had no idea what they'd be facing in Jordan other than she wouldn't be able to dress the same there, temperature and convention both playing an important role. She packed several loose cotton outfits, including scarves to cover her hair. It didn't matter whether you were religious or not in the Middle East. Women from everywhere, including American women, were expected to keep covered.

It was easier to comply instead of drawing extra attention, especially with the importance of their mission, so Zahara made sure both Cat and Evelyn had scarfs of their own to cover their heads. It was also the end of December all over the world. While she was certain it would be drier and hoped it was warmer than Scotland, it wasn't unheard of for Jordan to occasionally have snow at this time of year.

"Do you have everything you need, *jaani*?"

Zahara turned at the sound of her mum's quiet voice. "I have no idea. I hope so." She gestured to her bag. "It's hard to know what I'll need when I'm not even sure where I'm going to end up."

Her mum came into the room and sat on the bed beside her, then leaned in and gave her a hug, pausing to rest her head on Zahara's shoulder.

"All you require is a few clothes and some money. You can always call if you need anything else, or your friend Evelyn can contact us if you're somewhere you don't have access to phones." She stood, putting her hands on Zahara's shoulders and looking at her from arms-length. "My daughter. Such a strong woman you've become. You make me so proud."

Zahara felt the hot prickle of tears threatening to spill over and did her best to brush her mum's words aside. "I haven't done anything yet. Save your pride a little longer, okay?"

Her mum rolled her eyes at the protest, causing Zahara to snort. "Okay, fine. I accept your pride in me." She paused as an idea suddenly came to her. "There is one more thing I'd like to know before we leave, if you can tell me."

Her mum raised an eyebrow. "What's that?"

"Why is the spell failing now? Because of Reema's death?"

Her mum shrugged, looking away briefly before meeting her eyes again. When she finally did, Zahara wasn't expecting the hint of fear she saw even though she gave a cheerful non-answer.

"I'm not sure, sweetie. Maybe it's just time. Nothing lasts forever, after all."

Zahara shook her head. "No, that's not it. I think it's what you said earlier. It has something to do with Reema's death. Somehow, her dying and sending the amulet left us unprotected from the curse. That's why I have to take it back. But it's related to more than just this necklace, or Reema wouldn't have sent it away in the first place."

Her mum sighed. "I'm not sure about any of it but you could be right. The timing is suspect otherwise. Be careful who you talk to. Trust no one other than your friends, okay? The world beyond the boundaries you've known is strange and magical in a way you haven't been exposed to here. Magic is still strongly believed in away from the Western world, where fairy tales are mere stories most do not see as truth. In the desert, people believe in things beyond science. I'm worried someone will try to take advantage of you if they know what you have and what you are."

Zahara nodded. "I promise. We'll come back as quickly as possible. I'll be home this time next week. How does that sound?"

She smiled, brushing her daughter's hair off her face. "From your mouth to Allah's ear, *jaani*."

CAT AND EVELYN WERE waiting by the backdoor, packed and ready to go, when Zahara finally came out of her room.

"Ready?" Zahara asked, as she looped her backpack over her arms.

Cat nodded, flipping her long, red ponytail over her shoulder. "Ready as I'll ever be. I'm really excited about going to Petra to be honest. I haven't been anywhere remotely close to Jordan, and I'm looking forward to seeing the countryside."

Zahara smiled. Prior to their adventure a little over a year ago, Cat hadn't even left the United States. With the help of Robin, and in no small part due to the evil they were being forced to battle, Cat was getting the chance to do quite a bit of traveling since coming into her powers.

"Well, you've been to Norway. That's somewhere."

Cat waved her comment away. "Yeah, but that was almost like being in the States. Most people spoke English. Sometimes I could pretend I was on the west coast, somewhere rural. This is going to be way different. I'm looking forward to seeing Petra in real life. The pictures I've seen are breathtaking, so it must be even better up close."

"Don't be too disappointed if things don't live up to your imagination, Cat," Evelyn warned her. "I hear there's been a lot of vandalism in the last few years, including damage from a few terrorist attacks."

Cat rolled her eyes. "Just let me have my excitement, okay? I'm sure we're headed into another battle between good and evil, but I want to pretend I'm a real tourist for ten seconds."

Zahara laughed. "Wow, you guys are sounding more related by the day!"

She watched as Cat, with her long red hair, blue eyes, pale complexion, and near-giantess height of five foot, ten inches, looked six inches down toward Evelyn, with her tawny skin, curly dark hair, and deep brown eyes.

Evelyn smirked. "Yeah, we're practically twins."

Zahara shrugged, unconcerned about the dry response. "Well, for a minute I thought I was listening to Cat and Vanessa fight. Apparently, the longer you're friends with someone, the more you start to sound like sisters."

Evelyn chuckled, not upset in the least. "Fine, you've pegged us. Now, let's get going. I want to see if we can find a good place to set up a base camp while we figure out what to do next."

Nodding, Zahara led the way to the gazebo. The familiar shimmer of light marked the entrance from the backyard into Summerland, and they stepped across the threshold into the glade on the other side.

Looking around the peaceful scene in front of them, they waited a few minutes until a young man appeared, smiling as he held his arms out to them.

"Ladies!" Robin graced them with a deep bow. "It's wonderful to see you again so soon. Are you ready to travel?"

Evelyn greeted him with a lingering kiss. Cat and Zahara gave each other a look then averted their eyes as they waited for them to finish saying hello.

"Yes, my love. We're ready. Where are we going?" Evelyn stepped back, running her hands down his bare chest in a brief caress.

Robin in any form preferred to wear as little clothing as he could. When he was an eight-year-old, it wasn't a big deal to see him running around with a pair of shorts on. As a handsome, partially clothed twenty-something with washboard abs, it was more disconcerting. Zahara tried to hide her blush.

"My friend, Omar, is waiting on the other side. There is a green space you will see when you step through. He will be there with the necessary supplies."

Zahara cleared her throat, still distracted by the shirtless Robin. "I had another question I was hoping you'd be able to answer."

Robin flashed her a smile. "What is that, my little fox?

"Why is the curse coming for my family now? If what my mum says is true, it's been over five hundred years."

Robin looked up to the sky as he sighed. "I believe you have already deduced the answer."

She nodded. "When my aunt died, the spell failed, didn't it?"

Robin looked sad. "When Reema's power began to falter, all of this was set in motion. It is the reason you have the amulet now, and also why you must go back. You need to return the amulet to the origin of the spell and recast it."

"Recast it? How?"

Robin shrugged. "I do not have all the answers. I just know you must go to Petra and take the amulet with you. You will need to be careful, because the Guardian of the land is absent."

Evelyn looked at Robin suspiciously. "Wait just a minute. What exactly are you saying?"

Robin gave Evelyn a weak smile, one Zahara recognized from when her dad was in her mum's bad books. "Um, yes, I may have forgotten to mention it. The area you are going is currently unguarded."

"Does that mean..." Zahara started, then stopped.

Robin nodded. "Yes, it means that unlike here, where I am able to protect you from most evil, you will be on your own once you arrive. I have a few friends who will be able to guide you, but no one able to defeat a being as powerful as the jinn. My powers are weaker away from the British Isles, but I will help when possible. You must rely on each other, as well as the friends you will meet along the way."

Robin squeezed Zahara's shoulder the way her mum had earlier that morning and the same wave of reassurance flooded her now.

He let go, saluted Cat, then planted a quick kiss on Evelyn's cheek before he bowed again. "I will see you all later. Good luck."

A small breeze kicked up and a cloud of dandelion fluff appeared, hiding him from view. When it descended again, he was gone.

Zahara turned to Cat and Evelyn with a rueful expression. "Well, that's encouraging. I guess that means it's time to go?"

Evelyn held her head high. "It's time. I see a doorway, over to the left of that tree. Let's head over."

Together, they walked toward the doorway. Instead of the usual tree or hill they'd most often found a gate in the past, in between the trees there was a smooth sandstone arch. It was a rich ochre, ornately carved with images Zahara didn't recognize. Some appeared to be Arabic letters and numbers, while others were so highly stylized she couldn't decipher them.

As she stepped through the arch, she felt the familiar tingle that always reminded her of static electricity coat her body. When she opened her eyes, she was standing in a green, shrub covered area with her friends right beside her.

Cat's eyebrows were drawn together in a puzzled expression as she examined the bush next to her. She turned to Zahara. "Did we go to the right place?"

"I have no idea. Robin said we'd come to a park of some sort. So, maybe?"

Zahara hadn't thought to see this much in the way of green either, given they were supposed to be arriving in the desert. But he had mentioned a green space. As she examined the area around her, it seemed likely this was where he'd meant.

While her initial reaction had been one of lush greenery, the longer she observed the more desert-like the landscape became. The ground was covered in green, yes, but small green shrubs, not trees like at home. Underneath the shrubs, the ground was a mixture of gravel and something that appeared to be cold lava. As she surveyed the land, she realized that they were standing on an ancient volcanic plain.

"This is different from what I expected." Evelyn crouched to pick up one of the dark stones then stood and pointed to something just behind Zahara. "Do you think he's our guide?"

Zahara whipped around, grabbing her scarf and smoothly covering her hair in one fluid movement as she turned. Walking toward them from behind a Jeep she swore hadn't been there a minute earlier was a guy around the same age they were.

Crinkles formed at the corner of his eyes as he smiled, revealing a dimple in one cheek that reminded her a little of her brother, Suf, when he was up to mischief.

"Hello. Are you Zahara?"

His voice was a warm baritone with a hint of accent and Zahara felt her cheeks tingle and warm.

Well, that's unexpectedly awkward.

"Hello, yes. I'm Zahara. These are my friends, Cat and Evelyn. Are you Omar?"

He bobbed his head. "I am. Robin asked me to show you to the starting point. We have arranged to camp nearby tonight, but you will need to travel further to get there. Please, allow me to assist you to your destination. It isn't a long drive, but it is much too far to walk from here."

He gestured to the waiting Jeep and began to walk toward it.

"Thank you." Zahara heard her voice crack slightly and quickly cleared her throat.

She was unexpectedly nervous around this man, which was odd, considering how comfortable she was around most people. She wondered what it meant, but didn't think he was dangerous. Especially if Robin had sent him to help them.

Plus, she didn't get any of the uncomfortable creepy feelings she usually did when someone wasn't to be trusted. She didn't have the abilities Cat or Evelyn had to see auras, but her animal instincts about humans hadn't let her down yet.

Zahara followed him to the Jeep, checking once to ensure Cat and Evelyn were behind her, before sitting down next to him in the front seat.

"So, how'd you score this duty?" Evelyn asked from behind Omar as she fastened her seat belt.

Omar laughed as he turned to answer her question. "Oh, Robin and I go way back." He paused, wiggling his eyebrows. "He helped me out with some nasty business involving the Brits and the Turks a few decades ago." He smiled at Zahara, raising an eyebrow at her confused look. "You'd know all about that, wouldn't you? They can be nasty at times for such proper blokes."

Zahara was surprised to hear such a Britishism coming from him but was more curious about the event he was referring to. "What are you talking about?"

Omar shrugged before giving her a sheepish smile. "Oh, good ol' T. E. Lawrence. He was fine, but some of the other British officers weren't so kind to the local boys, back in the day. But that was another battle in another time, as they say."

Cat wrinkled her brow. "Wait, T. E. Lawrence? *The* Lawrence of Arabia."

Omar scoffed. "Well, I guess that *would* be how he's remembered. He always was a bit of a show off."

"But that would make you..." Cat trailed off, eyes widening.

Zahara did the math in her head. "At least one hundred or..."

She searched his smooth, unlined face for evidence of age beyond the superficial early twenties that she'd assumed, but saw nothing. He still looked a year or two older than her at most.

He bent his neck in a tiny nod of acknowledgement as he turned the engine on and began to drive. As he smoothly maneuvered the vehicle over the dips in the road, he answered. "Give or take, yes. My family is a long-lived bunch. We are closely tied to this land and the magic within it. That connection allows us to age more slowly than most, unless we leave to visit other places. If we stay away for any length of time, we begin to age at the same rate as everyone else."

Zahara nodded. "That explains how you knew Lawrence of Arabia personally. And Robin?"

Omar nodded but didn't take his eyes off the road. "I know the area, as well as those who've visited, because I've been here so long. I'll help you as much as I can, but from what Robin has explained, this will just be the jumping off point. You need to head to Amman, the capital city of Jordan, next. From there, it's an easy drive to Petra. I'll take you to the campsite tonight so we can plan the next few days. In the morning, I'll take you to Amman to get supplies for Petra."

Zahara watched as he drove down the vague suggestion of road, fascinated by the small amount of personal information he'd shared. He spoke of the land as they drove, and now she knew they were in a protected volcanic spill-off area, she wasn't sure they were supposed to be driving through it at all.

But even more than her awe of the harsh and beautiful landscape, Zahara found herself unable to look away from the man driving. After the initial surprise and blushing, she'd managed to control her expression and her color had returned to normal. She knew better than most how to hide reactions, after growing up with three brothers who thrived on embarrassing her.

But the strange curiosity to know more about him was still there and seemed to be growing by the minute. She was so captivated she jerked when the Jeep stopped in front of a roomy, rectangular tent.

"We're here. Bring all your bags in. We'll stay here tonight, so that you ladies can have a chance to experience true Bedouin life." Omar's eyes flashed in a lively fashion. "Which includes a nice cup of Arabian coffee, of course."

They disembarked and hoisted their backpacks over their shoulders, following Omar into a tent that looked straight out of *1001 Arabian Nights*. It wasn't made from the usual pre-fab nylon design she was accustomed to rather it looked as if someone had hand-made the material from thick burlap. Inside, the floors were covered with rich carpets which gave it an unexpected homeyness. The instant Zahara stepped inside, she felt a welcome sense of belonging and the stress of living in a busy city faded behind her.

I could get used to this.

Omar put a kettle on a small stove in the corner and began to boil the water. "Anyone in the mood for coffee? It's traditional Arabic style, which means we add a little cardamom and saffron. I can also make it plain, if you'd prefer."

"However you make it is lovely, thank you."

Evelyn came up behind Zahara, giving her a knowing look. "Are you enjoying the view, Z?"

Zahara flushed. She knew exactly what her no-nonsense friend was hinting at but didn't know how to answer. She didn't want to think about her weird reaction to him with everything else she was supposed to be figuring out.

"Yes, it's a very nice *tent*."

She lifted her chin stubbornly at Evelyn's raised eyebrow, but luckily her friend didn't push her any further.

"Yes, such a nice tent! I'm looking forward to sleeping here tonight." Cat agreed with Zahara, completely missing the quiet drama playing out between her friends due to her own excitement. "Just think, we'll be sleeping under the stars in a place the Bedouins have been for centuries. The same way they've been doing since who knows when." Cat's eyes widened further and she clapped her hands suddenly. "Just like T. E. Lawrence!"

Zahara laughed, amused by her friend's enthusiasm. It was a nice distraction from her own mixed feelings. "I'm glad you're glad. But it sounds like this is just a brief stop in our journey. We need to decide what we're doing next. We still have a little traveling to do before we get to Petra."

Omar overheard them. "Robin filled me in on the importance of your mission, so I was planning to start driving first thing in the morning. It will take us the whole day to drive to Amman, in order to skirt the border of Saudi." He smiled briefly. "Much easier than trying to explain your presence in the country. It is possible another gate would have been closer to Petra, but I was the only one available to assist you. Altogether, it's about a fourteen-hour drive to Amman from here."

Cat groaned. "That's so long!"

Omar shrugged. "It is, but hopefully the route we are taking will allow us to remain hidden and off the radar of the border securities, as well as unobserved by any creatures who may mean you harm."

He turned to look at Zahara, his expression solemn. He was standing close enough she could feel the warmth coming from his body, and again, a strange tingle spread over her.

"You will need to be on guard at all times, *hubun*."

Zahara didn't know the word Omar used, but the way he said it and the look on his face as he spoke made her wonder if it was an endearment, and she flushed again.

This time he noticed and his expression changed, shifting into something she couldn't read. Smiling abruptly, he once again became the cheerful host.

"Come! The coffee is ready. We shall sit down, and I will show you the maps. Some of them are quite old, so careful with your drinks please."

Zahara trailed behind Cat and Evelyn, taking a moment to watch as her friends sat at the small table close to the ground. The couches were low, with ample pillows. Cat bounced slightly, testing them, and smiled when Omar passed her a coffee. He moved to the other side of the table to give Evelyn her cup, and she found herself thinking her parents would approve of his easy hospitality.

She instantly scolded herself for the way she was looking at him. She didn't have time to indulge in thoughts of that nature.

Besides, he's already told us he can't leave his home without becoming decrepit. That's a relationship doomed before it starts— a guy who's multiple decades older than I am, who ages rapidly the minute he goes anywhere. And I thought the guys I was meeting were reluctant to leave home before!

Zahara sighed and sat down beside Cat, who smiled and patted her leg. Zahara leaned against her shoulder in relief as some of her tension vanished. Cat had the ability to read auras and heal people and hadn't missed the confusion swirling in her aura. The break from worry was appreciated, as was the fact Cat wouldn't say anything about her inner turmoil.

It was nice having someone who understood, and better yet, a friend who didn't blurt out your secrets. When Zahara caught Evelyn's eye though, she wasn't surprised when she received a wink in return.

While Evelyn couldn't read auras quite the same way Cat did, she was the acknowledged relationship expert of the group and didn't need to use any special abilities to sense Zahara's interest in their host.

Her friends were so different, but Zahara would never be able to choose between them if asked which one she liked more. Evelyn was bold and in your face, but kind; while Cat was quieter and empathic. She was so lucky they were here to help her with such an enormous undertaking.

Turning her attention to the maps in front of her with a sense of foreboding, Zahara knew this was the easy part of her quest. There was no doubt in her mind her turmoil would continue to grow from this point onward.

CHAPTER 6

Zahara slept under the stars in human form for the first time that night. Camping wasn't something she'd ever done, but it was cozy and peaceful inside the tent. Something about knowing the desert stars shone brightly outside their shelter in the calm night made her relax more than she'd thought possible in a strange land, especially under the circumstances.

Maybe it helped that before they had turned in for the night Omar revealed he'd put up guards against the supernatural. While she wasn't sure what he meant, the look of certainty on his face had translated well. Whether his disclosure contributed to her refreshing sleep or if it had been a product of the desert itself, by the time the morning sun woke her, she was filled with an unexpected sense of happiness.

She sat up from the ground level cot, feeling stiff in her clothes. Glancing over to find her friends still sleeping, she smiled. They'd all stayed up late the night before with the maps and decided against changing into pj's in the face of the chill of the night, but now she couldn't help thinking longingly about her shower at home. She resigned herself to the knowledge today was only the first of many mornings where she wouldn't have access to a shower.

The smell of coffee wafting through the air distracted her from her reverie at the same moment the sound of objects clattering in the small kitchen area made her prick up her ears. She turned to see Omar moving around, humming tunelessly to himself as he readied their breakfast of yoghurt, bread, and dates.

Taking a deep breath, she stood and brushed off her wrinkled shirt and pants. Grimacing at the lack of improvement her efforts produced she rolled her eyes and gave up, walking over to lean on the small table where they'd reviewed maps and planned their trip the night before.

"Good morning. I hope you slept well?" Omar smiled as he placed a platter of food in front of her then went to the kitchen again, returning a second time with two small cups of coffee. As he placed them down, he sat directly across from her and tilted his head, waiting for her to reply.

"Yes, thank you. It was almost as relaxing as sleeping in my true form."

Zahara stopped, wincing. It wasn't something she usually spoke of, but she'd been so at ease it had slipped out.

Omar looked at her with interest. "Your true form? Robin didn't share very much information about you and your friends, other than the importance of the quest you are undertaking. I would love to know more, if you are comfortable sharing, of course."

Zahara felt the same tingle of interest as he waited for her response. *Why not? It wasn't like he didn't have his own supernatural secrets if he was as old as he said.*

"I am most comfortable in my earth mage form. In my case, it resembles a small desert fennec fox. I do have some abilities

with earth magic, although I'm embarrassed to admit not nearly as much as my parents do."

"Oh?" His eyes were bright as he leaned forward.

Zahara shrugged, feeling unexpectedly defensive despite
his interest. "I live in a large city and don't practice as much as
I should. It was a trade-off, I guess—I love my parents and miss
them, but I needed to move out to find my own way."

Omar nodded, sipping from his coffee. He kept his eyes focused on her as he put his coffee down. "I understand. I left
home to find my own way as well, although that was many
years ago. Sadly, my parents have since passed away. I alone remain, along with a few cousins. I was an only child and times
were more difficult when I was young. Perhaps if I had been
born later, my parents would still be here for you to meet instead of being lost in the turmoil of war."

Zahara flushed, trying to hide both her embarrassment and
excitement with a bite of date. She chewed with intense concentration while she tried to decide what to say next. The possibility that he wanted her to meet his parents was...serious. Obviously, it couldn't happen if they were dead, but it made her
think about introducing her parents, which in turn made swal-
lowing the date more difficult. She took a sip of coffee and was
relieved when she managed to get it down without choking.

She was saved from death by awkwardness when Cat and
Evelyn joined them, sitting beside her on the couch.

"Hey!" Cat smiled, her white teeth nearly blinding.

Evelyn stifled a yawn. "Morning."

Zahara smiled at her friends opposing responses to the
morning. Over the time she'd known them, they'd shifted in
the way they greeted the day. At first, they'd both been slow

starters. But as Cat's powers had increased she'd become a true early bird while Evelyn, with her goddess of dreams role, had transitioned to more of a night owl.

Empathy flooded her at the bruises under Evelyn's eyes, and she got up to pour her friend a cup of coffee.

Evelyn accepted gratefully, sighing as the fragrance hit her nose. "Thanks, Zahara. It was a busy night."

Zahara nodded, feeling bad for her friend. Although Evelyn had come to help, it sounded like none of her other duties had been placed on hold. Cat patted Evelyn's shoulder and she watched Evelyn visibly perk up. Zahara knew Cat had given Evelyn a small hit of energy, the same way she'd done for her yesterday.

"Any dreams relating to what's ahead of us?" Cat asked.

Evelyn shook her head. "No, nothing last night about our trip. Just more of the usual."

Cat and Zahara exchanged glances. They knew most of Evelyn's free time was spent trouble-shooting problems she discovered in her dreams, and they both wished they could take away some of her burden.

Evelyn caught their sympathetic looks and objected immediately. "Woah. No poor Evelyn BS, okay? I signed up for this gig and I'm totally fine. You need to stop worrying about me, especially with the job we're supposed to be focusing on in the here and now. I'm fine, got it?"

Zahara nodded meekly at the stern look she shot them. It seemed to mollify Evelyn enough that she sat down, cradling her cup as though it held the nectar of the gods.

Turning to Omar to avoid further grumpy morning glares, Zahara asked something which had been nagging her. "After breakfast we'll be ready to leave, but should we need be watching out for anything while we travel? What about border security? Is there any potential for attacks along the road?"

"I have my own small amount of skill in remaining unseen." Omar said, smiling. "I can be as invisible as I want and extend it to our group during this trip, fear not. The biggest concern you will find is what happens if you drink too much coffee along the way. Places to relieve yourself can be few and far between, unless you are comfortable with small desert bushes."

Cat made a show of putting her coffee down and they all laughed. Within minutes, they were packed up and back in the Jeep. Zahara sat in the front again, with Cat and Evelyn in the back of the vehicle with the bags. They had looped their scarves loosely around their necks for warmth against the cool desert morning and Zahara sat back to watch the sun rise with silent appreciation.

AT FIRST, THEY ENJOYED the scenery, with the occasional comment on the stark desert and scrub landscape breaking the quiet. After a few hours of the same though, it had become monotonous and they dozed off, one by one. When Zahara woke up after a short cat-nap, she looked back to discover both of her friends sleeping.

Omar noticed she was awake and held a bag of dates out to her. Smiling her thanks, she took one and bit it, gazing out the window. To her left was a wide expanse of water, which felt somewhat out of place after all the desert.

"Is that the ocean?"

"That is the Red Sea. I took the overland pass earlier but looped around to avoid an area that can sometimes be troublesome. We should be in Amman in about three hours. You will have plenty of time to rest more once we get there."

Omar flashed her another warm smile she couldn't help returning. His gaze lingered just long enough she felt a flush start to creep over her cheeks.

Ugh. I can't believe how immature I'm being. It's not like I haven't spent time with a guy I wasn't related to before. But he seems different. I wish I knew more about him but sadly, duty comes first.

To distract herself, she looked out of her window again. The contrast between the sea on one side and desert on the other was brilliant and helped a little.

"What do you think?"

Omar's soft question intruded on her attempt to ignore how she felt next to him and made her realize she wasn't doing a very good job distracting herself at all.

"About what?" Her throat was suddenly as parched as the desert.

"About the landscape. It's beautiful, isn't it?" He glanced at the sea to his left.

It felt odd being on the wrong side of the road, and she realized this could be part of why her friends were so jumpy when she drove them around in the UK. Or maybe it was her driving. Either way, she agreed with him.

"It's quite striking." She paused, and after checking her friends weren't listening, cleared her throat. "Omar, I know we asked how old you were, but you didn't really answer. You just said you'd been around during the First World War. Do you mind if I ask again? I'm curious, if you don't think it's inappropriate."

She hoped it wasn't rude, but the idea of everything he must have seen if he was over a hundred years old was fascinating. It was difficult to reconcile the handsome man driving with someone older than her *dādā*.

He sighed and turned his head, giving her a rueful smile. "It's not inappropriate but it is hard to answer. I was in my early teens when T.E. came to our village. My father and cousins helped him fight against the Turks. They were responsible for destroying the railway so the Turkish army had to rebuild it to get across, a pivotal event in the success of the people at defeating the Ottomans. But the actual year I was born is more challenging as paper records weren't always accurate. It was after 1900, maybe 1903 or 4. I was only about twelve or thirteen when T.E. came to our village."

His face was wistful as he drove, and Zahara could tell the memories were difficult but didn't know what to say to make it better. "That must have been hard."

Even as the words escaped, she shook her head at how insufficient they were. He smiled, luckily appearing unaware he was talking to someone who wasn't good at conversation.

"He was a great man. There is more I could tell you about him that will never show up in any history book. So many accounts were lost during the years of war, but that was just life back then." He shrugged. "Man has always struggled against man. Whether because of injustice, greed, or power. As magical beings, we've been no better and have often been as swept up in the winds of change as they are."

He smiled, his face losing the wistful look as he sharpened his attention on her. Her eyes widened in alarm as he changed the subject.

"That is all ancient history. I'd much rather learn about you. You mentioned you live in a city? Is it hard for you, being an earth mage surrounded by bricks and mortar?"

He glanced briefly at her face before turning his concentration toward the road again, missing her half-shrug in response.

"Sometimes. I live close to some green spaces and I spend most of my free time at my parents' on weekends. It helps me relax and reconnect with my magic. While I love the excitement of the city and the freedom of being my own person, I do miss the connection to the earth when I'm there. It isn't the same."

"Yes, I imagine it wouldn't be. Well, maybe after this trip you'll have a chance to reexamine your situation. Who knows? Maybe the city won't be your only option."

"Maybe," she agreed.

She watched him as he drove, curious about his cryptic words. He'd said them so offhandedly they shouldn't have stuck with her, but something in his tone set off small alarms in her head and the conversation faltered.

Even as she decided she was totally overthinking things, she couldn't stop dwelling on his words. Living in Edinburgh had always seemed her only way out from the quaint town she'd grown up near. Life on the farm had been constricting at times, even if her magic required a close connection with the earth.

As she looked at the vast spaces of the desert around her now, she found herself considering what being an earth mage really meant. Obviously, her family wasn't tied to a specific area of land the way Omar's needed to be. They'd moved first to Pakistan, and from there to the UK. What if moving further away from her family was an option? If it was, it was one she'd never considered before.

"Are we there yet?" Evelyn's sleepy yawn made her words hardly understandable as she stretched in the backseat. "Oh. This isn't a city. Where are we?"

Omar smiled at her briefly via the rearview mirror. "We are over halfway there, likely three or so more hours of driving, depending on road conditions. I was thinking we could stop for a picnic shortly. There's a shady area where caravans rest just up ahead." He chuckled. "While we aren't a caravan, it will serve us just as well."

Their conversation woke Cat, who yawned before adding her two cents. "That sounds good. I'm hungry."

Zahara laughed. "You and your sister are practically insatiable."

Cat gave her a proud grin. "It's in the genes, I guess."

"Well, don't worry. I brought enough food for ten people." Omar's certainty faltered as he caught Zahara's expression. "That will that be enough, no?"

Zahara shrugged, barely repressing a smirk. "I'll eat less if she needs more."

Cat tapped her on the shoulder. "Excuse me! I'm not a greedy monster. I share."

Zahara winked. "I know you do."

Omar slowed and pulled over to the side of the road. There were a few other cars stopped in a rough parking lot area with signs. It was empty as Zahara got out, and she paused in awe at the sight of the large red rocks in the distance. She could sense the power coming out of the ground from here and exhaled as it washed over her.

"Where are we?"

Omar's face had softened as he regarded the view and he turned to Zahara with a contemplative expression. "This area is called Wadi Rum. The rocks in the distance are the Seven Pillars of Wisdom, which you may have heard about in movies and books about T.E. Lawrence. This entire area is sacred to the Bedouins."

"It's magnificent."

"I see it is speaking to you."

Zahara nodded absently, taking a few steps toward the rocks with her hand outstretched before stopping and sucking in a breath. Energy seemed to pulse inside her, like a heartbeat in sync with her own. She felt strangely powerful in that moment, as if she could call up whatever she needed to from the ground and it would be hers.

Her friends came to stand beside her and Evelyn placed a hand on her shoulder. "This is your place, isn't it?"

Zahara frowned. "My place? What do you mean?"

She gestured toward the rocks in the distance. "This place speaks to your soul. We all have a place that hits us like this. You don't remember watching Cat walk around Edinburgh with big eyes? When she was cursing her ancestors for leaving such a beautiful place?"

Zahara nodded, looking at Cat in time to catch a faraway look enter her eyes.

"Edinburgh is so great. I wish I could live there."

"See? That's what I mean. This place does the same thing for you."

"It's so weird. I've never been here before but it pulls at me. It feels like home somehow, even from this far away."

Omar came closer, leaning to point over her shoulder toward the pillars. "This area was home to Bedouins long before written history. If we were to go closer, you would see wall paintings and old trails cutting through the rocks. If you wish, when you have completed your quest, I will show you. This is my family's ancestral home. I am very proud of it and love showing it to those who appreciate its beauty as much as I do."

He looked down at Zahara, now only a few inches away. Her throat closed, making it impossible to reply. His dark eyes were warm, his breath close enough to feel a light tickle against her cheek. In that moment, in this place, she felt connected to him as well.

For an instant, the world stopped.

She wasn't sure how long they stood frozen in place before his arm slowly fell to his side. She would have stayed longer, but their interlude was broken when Cat groaned and dramatically clasped her stomach.

"Can we eat now? I'm really, really hungry."

Why am I reacting like this? Zahara turned away, oddly shaky inside as she looked away, but when she looked at her friend pretending to be dying of hunger, her confusion was replaced by laughter and she shook her head.

"Are you taking acting lessons from your sister? Since when did you start becoming so dramatic?" Zahara stole a quick peek at Omar but looked away quickly when she caught him watching her with an inscrutable expression.

Cat patted her stomach again. "Sorry, Zahara. I think I got the weaker version of the drama gene; it's only activated at meal times."

Evelyn laughed at the gesture. "You don't want to be around either sister when they're hungry if you aren't near a food source. It's loud, frightening, and sometimes makes me wonder if they've ever fought over shoe leather."

Omar chuckled as he made a show of quickly pulling a cooler out of the back of the Jeep, turning to Cat with a mock-terrified grimace. "I'm becoming worried for my own safety. If you allow me a minute to set up, I'll back away slowly, I promise."

Cat, Evelyn, and Zahara helped as he unfolded a blanket for them to sit on, then pulled out a spread of meat, cheese, bread, and dates. They ate in silence, due to combination of hunger and their eagerness to get back on the road.

As they cleaned up the remains of the meal, Zahara took one last, longing glance at the landscape before shuffling back to the vehicle. Something in her face must have betrayed her sadness as she did up her seatbelt because when Omar sat beside her, he reached over to touch her arm with a lightness she hadn't expected.

"I understand. Every time I come here I have to force myself to leave. I feel the strongest here and the most at peace. I promise, I will bring you back as soon as it's safe."

Zahara nodded at the look in his eyes. She knew he would bring her back, but she heard more than mere words. In his voice was the vow of his time as well.

As they drove away, there was nothing in the world she wanted more than a chance to explore Wadi Rum with him.

CHAPTER 7

The landscape changed as they drove from the scarcely occupied roughness of sand to a city populated with a variety of dwellings. When they entered Amman a few hours later, Zahara was struck by how different the buildings were from those at home.

It wasn't so much the crowding as it was the way they appeared to be building blocks instead of buildings. Some were sand-colored, others shone bright white, especially as they entered the business area. When they came to the older part of the city, she noticed bricks and stairs on the sides of houses and had a brief sensation of disorientation as she realized these houses may have looked the same a thousand years ago. They would probably look the same a thousand years from now.

People went about their daily business in a wide variety of dress; all the way from what she considered the more traditional Arabic style to the Western look she was accustomed to seeing at home. Most women wore some form of head covering, but she did see a few tourists walking around uncovered. Zahara pulled her scarf up, tucking her hair in. Even though she was from the West, she knew it was proper to remain covered.

"We're here." Omar parked the Jeep on the street in an open space, casually smiling at the girls. "You aren't required to cover up in this neighborhood, but you will draw less attention if you do."

Cat and Evelyn nodded and pulled their scarves up as well.

"Women have a more freedom in Jordan than in Saudi, but it's still best to dress modestly and match the area you're in. One thing I want to mention before I forget is to be careful about touching people of the opposite sex in public. It's frowned on even though Jordan is more relaxed about these things."

Cat gave Evelyn a knowing look, but she just smirked.

"That's not going to be a problem. Robin's nowhere around."

Zahara rolled her eyes at their teasing but was relieved. It was sometimes awkward to watch as Robin and Evelyn expressed their affection so easily in public. Public displays of affection definitely had huge cultural variations. Yet, at the same time she was relieved a being spared the PDA so comfortable to Evelyn, part of her wondered what it would be like to have that in a relationship— to be free to touch someone else as if they were an extension of yourself.

Her eyes flew to Omar before she could stop herself and she caught him watching her, his gaze lingering, then sharpening with interest as the familiar heat rose in her face. He glanced away at the same time she did.

Turning to the building beside them, he cleared his throat. "Um...we'll be staying here tonight. It's been a long day already so we'll get supplies tomorrow before heading to Petra. We can buy food once we get there but the selection is better here. Because you don't know how long you'll be staying, I will purchase enough for a week if that sounds reasonable?"

Zahara nodded as she averted her gaze, pretending to fiddle with the strap on her backpack while she attempted to regain some of her composure. Her plan failed miserably when he reached out to help.

"Would you like a hand with that?"

Zahara shook her head and flashed a bright smile, trying to play it cool. "No, thank you. I've got it."

"You have beautiful eyes." He blinked, then clapped his hands together, and turned to face Cat and Evelyn. "Follow me. Our apartment is upstairs."

By the time Zahara reached the landing on the third floor, she was having a hard time catching her breath. How much of it was from the way she was beginning to feel around Omar versus the stairs themselves wasn't clear to her. As much as she cursed the way they'd met and the timing, she knew if it wasn't for her quest to return the amulet she likely wouldn't have crossed paths with him at all.

Could this be another part of the challenge? Another obstacle to overcome?

She focused on catching her breath as she waited for him to unlock the door to the apartment. She didn't want to seem quite as out of shape as she was sure she looked. She followed the others in, taking in the simple apartment with curiosity.

When he caught her examining a picture of a family, he smiled at the confusion on her face. "This is a family home, belonging to my cousins and I. We all are permitted use it when we need to be in the city for supplies or other reasons. None of my relatives enjoy living in a city, so it frequently remains unoccupied. Amman has always been an important trading center in the area. Luckily for us, it isn't far from our traditional desert home and therefore doesn't cause too much distress to stay here for short periods of time. Other than the usual irritations which come with city living, of course."

Zahara took in his words as she walked around, looking at the decorations. It was sparse but comfortable with thick and ornate Persian rugs on the floor in front of a small red couch in the large communal area. The main room was set up like a traditional living room, but she could see two hallways branching off to either side.

One led to a kitchen, which Omar showed them briefly before taking them down the other hall. He turned on the light to the bathroom before walking to another room and turning the light on there.

"You can share this room. I'm in the one at the end of the hall." He pointed at one of the two doors at the end before crossing his arms. "I will have food ready for six sharp in the morning. Please be on time if you wish to see Petra at its best. If you want to freshen up now, I will make us a light supper. After we are done eating, I recommend an early night. Petra is beautiful but very spacious. You'll need your energy for tomorrow, else it will feel even longer than today."

They thanked him and took his suggestion to heart, placing their bags in the room before eating a quick meal of sandwiches and pop. The cans of soda amused them all greatly, as the words *Pepsi* and *Coke* were written in Arabic, and if it hadn't been for the colors of the cans, they wouldn't have recognized the brand at all.

Cat yawned midway through the meal, covering her mouth with surprise. "Sorry, guys. I think Omar may be right. Are you ready for sleep? Because now that my tummy's full, I'm dead on my feet."

Zahara covered her mouth as she stifled her own yawn. They were contagious. "I'm not too bad. I didn't nap nearly as long as you two, but I'm sure you're more jet lagged than I am."

They ate and tidied up their mess, then took Omar's advice about an early night. When Zahara closed her eyes, instead of the nightmares she'd been having since learning of her mission, she dreamt of Wadi Rum and Omar smiling down at her.

THE MORNING SUN WAS weak and had hardly even made it into the sky when Cat's travel alarm rudely interrupted Zahara's dreams. She groaned and rolled over, trying to return to the red desert rocks, but it was too late. The scene had disappeared the way all good dreams did, leaving her with only the vaguest whisp to remember it by.

She sat up and swung her legs over the side of the bunk bed she'd slept on. Cat and Evelyn were on the bunks across from her and when she looked over, she found Cat was already wide awake. She compared her to Evelyn on the top bunk, who was currently imitating an immobile lump.

When Cat saw Zahara's eyes open, she used the flat of her hand to bang on the bottom of the upper bunk while crooning in a sing-song voice. "Oh, Evelyn, it's time to wake u-p."

It was easy to see which friend was more eager to get moving. It took a minute, but soon the sound of muttered cursing followed each of the taps. Cat stopped immediately, giving Zahara a mischievous look.

"Welp, that seems to have worked. Any bets on what she'll do to me?"

Evelyn's head appeared over the side, looking at her with a death glare. "You know how much I hate mornings."

Cat shrugged. "Yup, I do. Not much we can do about it though. Omar said we needed to be good to go for six so I set my alarm for 5:30 to give you enough time to get ready."

At Evelyn's continued glare and lack of coherent response, Cat smiled brightly and blew a kiss up to her as she sang, "You're welcome."

Zahara got out of bed, shaking her head as Cat looked to her for assistance. No way was she getting on Evelyn's bad side, even if they had somewhere to be. She was still nervous at the amount of power she'd seen from Evelyn in Scotland. The way she'd lit up and basically absorbed an ancient witch like Carman had been beyond human, or even elemental. It was the only time she'd seen her in action, but she wasn't eager to have an angry Evelyn direct that ability toward her.

She grabbed her toiletry bag and left her friends to their morning squabble, freshening up with a quick shower after she recalled Omar mentioning the more simple conditions he'd be taking them to. She was tempted to linger in the warmth, but didn't want to slow the others down.

By the time she returned to the room, Evelyn was glum but calm, and Cat had her bag packed and ready. She waited as her friends each took a turn through the bathroom, then they headed to the kitchen together where Omar was waiting with breakfast already made.

"Good morning! Grab a plate and dish up. I prepared plenty, as it will be a few hours until we get there. If I recall correctly, Cat requires large amounts of replenishments."

Cat beamed as she sat and began filling a plate. "Yes, sir! That's an order I can accommodate."

He laughed. "Perfect. Once you're full, we'll resupply at the grocery store down the street and be on our way."

Zahara took a plate and filled it, all the while wishing she could be as cheerful as Cat. The food looked good, but she ate mechanically. Her comforting dreams of the night before had vanished to be replaced by the reason they were going to Petra. The knowledge she may come face to face with evil sooner than she wanted to made it hard to enjoy the taste of what appeared to be a delicious spread.

After a few bites, she gave up and put her spoon down. "How safe are we?"

Omar looked at her, drawing his eyebrows together, then looked away. "I'm not sure. Robin only told me a jinn has a *eada*, a feud, against your family. That is bad, under any circumstances. The fact this is a jinn from the past makes it even worse."

Zahara pursed her lips. "Why would it be worse? Because he's old?"

Omar tilted his head. "Partly. The older a being of magic becomes, the stronger their power can grow. But the other reason to be concerned is because it is extremely rare to come across a full-blood jinn now. I've never met one."

Evelyn raised an eyebrow. "What do you mean?"

He gestured to Zahara, then to himself. "We both have the blood of jinn in our family lines. It is the source of our earth powers and the reason we are able to do what we can. Now, imagine the power of a creature without the weakness of humanity and mortality to temper their enormous power. Then add in the lack of restraint emotions such as love and friendship provide to tip power toward goodness and away from focusing only on what a creature desires."

Cat looked at her earnestly. "You know we're here to help you with anything you need."

"I'll protect you with my last breath," Evelyn agreed.

Zahara smiled weakly. It made her feel safer to have a goddess and a phoenix protecting her, but Omar's words burrowed into her mind, watering the seed of anxiety she'd so far managed to shove down since leaving Scotland.

"Thanks, guys. That means a lot." Zahara looked at Omar. "We'll be careful, but I expected it to be dangerous. Is there anything we need to watch for specifically? The more prepared I am, the better."

He shook his head. "Maybe one thing. Robin mentioned this jinn can manipulate reality. So if things start to look all weird or time begins moving funny, get out of there immediately."

Zahara nodded, pushing her food away. "That helps. I'm sorry, but I've lost my appetite."

She got up and took her plate to the sink to begin clearing up, but Omar stopped her with a light touch on the shoulder. Pleasant fire exploded, radiating from the center of the point of contact before he lifted his hand and stared.

His hand hovered for a second, dropping as he spoke. "Don't worry about this. Finish getting ready. I'll tidy up here."

Zahara nodded, feeling like she'd lost all control of speech. Her tongue had somehow become stuck to the roof of her mouth so without a word, she escaped past the curious and amused looks of Cat and Evelyn.

She sat on the bed with her eyes closed, breathing slowly in an attempt to regroup. Her emotions were all over the place. It had been enough trying to handle the fear and anxiety around the unknown situation she was walking into, but she wasn't at all prepared to deal with the potential of a romantic involvement with Omar.

Why now?

The click of the door opening caused her to startle and she turned as her friends entered.

"Okay, what was that?" Evelyn sat on Cat's bed, crossing her arms and tilting her head so she seemed to be looking down her nose at Zahara from across the room.

Zahara had the strangest sensation she was a little kid again as she shrugged helplessly. "I don't know. I feel so stupid whenever he's near. It's like I lose all ability to talk." She waved a hand around. "I've never lost the ability to talk. Just ask my family. And it's weird—I don't feel at all well near him. It's like I keep catching a sudden fever or something."

Evelyn nodded, pursing her lips as she tried to hide a smile. "Oh, girl. You're done for."

Cat laughed, sitting down beside Evelyn and swatting her arm. "Don't frighten the woman like that!" she admonished, then smiled at Zahara. "I'm not sure you're done for but it does sound like you may have a crush on him. That's not a bad thing. He seems like a great guy and he's got a similar background as you. That should make your parents happy, no?"

Zahara sighed. "No, it's not a bad thing. He *does* seem nice and Robin likes him, so that's huge. But the timing is awful. How am I going to get to know him better if I have to fight an evil jinn? Even if I win and return the amulet and everything goes back to normal, we'll still have a huge distance between us. Not to mention the little detail of him needing to be interested in me back for anything to happen."

At that, her friends burst into laughter.

Frowning, Zahara tilted her head. "What? What's so funny?"

Evelyn snorted. "Oh God, you sound like a heroine in a teen movie. Duh. Of course it's mutual. You guys keep staring randomly off into space or at each other."

Cat agreed. "Seriously Zahara, you may have bigger issues to deal with, but a lack of interest from him isn't one of your problems. So, let us help you get that amulet back to where it belongs so you can figure the more fun stuff out. Sound like a plan?"

Zahara smiled. She could always trust Cat's optimism to make things sound easy.

"Sounds like a plan."

CHAPTER 8

To their surprise, Omar had already loaded the Jeep with supplies by the time they were ready. It must have taken them longer than they realized but when Cat asked about it, he brushed it off.

"I called in a favor. A friend of mine let me get what we needed before the stores opened, so I decided to save some time. Everyone ready?"

They nodded in unison and he smiled.

"Perfect! Hop in and enjoy the ride."

It was a cool morning, and Zahara was happy to have her hair and throat covered by the scarf she'd wrapped around her head. Even though Omar had assured them Petra was full of tourists so the dress code didn't need to apply, they had dressed for warmth and with modesty in mind. Along with the scarf, she was also wearing a sweater and jacket.

She thought back to her decision to not take up the hijab when she'd entered puberty and felt a twinge. In the UK, it hadn't appealed to her, but for some reason, she felt comfortable wearing it now. Things were different here. For the first time, she wondered how many of her decisions were based on fitting in instead of what she actually believed. It was something she would have to examine when and if she went home. Maybe she'd reconsider her opinions.

"We'll be backtracking a little bit from our drive yesterday, but it's only about three hours. Wadi Musa is the nearest town to Petra. Technically, we could have stayed there. It has everything you need, but I find them much more expensive due to the tourist attractions in the area. And of course, I had a free place to stay in Amman." Omar kept his eyes on the road as he maneuvered the Jeep through traffic. "Enjoy the scenery while it lasts. We'll be there before lunch."

Zahara looked out her side window most of the way, torn between anxiety about the unknown threat looming closer and her desire to watch Omar as he drove. Since she couldn't decide which was stressing her out more, she watched as the desert slowly gave way to a bustling little town, then to a valley which led to the red sandstone she'd expected.

Zahara held her breath as they parked. The rocks seemed to spring straight up out of the sand in varying colors of brown, tan, and red. She wanted to get out and explore every inch even before the Jeep had come to a complete stop.

"This is amazing!" Cat exclaimed from behind her shoulder. "I can't wait to see everything. Omar, is it safe for us to get out and walk around?"

Zahara turned to catch his diffident shrug.

"Sure. I don't know where you are supposed to be looking, or what you need to watch out for. Robin's main directive for me was to get you here safely. The rest is up to you."

Zahara undid her seat belt and moved to open the door until he cleared his throat and stopped her.

"I have to leave you here for a bit. I have business to attend to in Wadi Musa. I wish I could stay, but..."

He trailed off, searching her eyes, then reached over. To her surprise, he gently took her hand in his and gave it a light squeeze. Her throat went dry.

"Please, be careful and stay safe, so that I can come back for you tonight."

"I'll try," she croaked, sounding more like a frog than a fox.

He didn't seem to notice as he squeezed her hand once more. "I'll come back at five. You can meet me at the treasury." He let go, looking reluctant as he turned to smile at Cat and Evelyn in the backseat. "Take good care of each other. I'll get the food for you to carry in your bags for the day. When I return tonight, I'll take you to the hotel in Wadi Musa."

Evelyn winked. "Don't worry, Omar, we'll keep her safe for you."

Zahara was amazed to see a red glow spreading over Omar's cheeks at her friend's usual brashness. Suddenly, she felt a lot more positive.

Maybe Cat and Evelyn were right about my feelings being reciprocated.

She got out of the Jeep with a slight spring in her step and waited as Omar filled them up with supplies. When he was finished, he waved a jaunty goodbye that didn't quite cover the worry in his eyes and drove away, leaving the three friends looking at each other.

Zahara turned to the awe-inspiring landscape and took a deep breath. "Ready?"

"So ready!" said Cat, more excited than anyone else as she bounced her backpack on.

As a history major, she'd talked nonstop about the Nabateans who had built in the rocks over two thousand years ago, so it wasn't a surprise when she began to elaborate on the history of Petra.

"This place has been settled for, like, forever."

Zahara and Evelyn shared a look. Zahara knew Cat was just warming up. At least her knowledge might turn out to be useful. So instead of tuning her out, Zahara listened closely.

"An earthquake in 365 AD caused the Nabatean kingdom to mostly abandon the settlement when it took out their water supply. Apparently, it was every bit as amazing as the Roman aqueducts until then."

Zahara nodded but kept her eyes on the scenery around them. "Go on. So, after the earthquake, Petra was abandoned?"

Cat shook her head. "No, Bedouins remained in the nearby area. They did occasionally camp inside the surviving structures, but the city was never the same afterward. It wasn't used much outside of that until the Arab revolt against the Ottomans."

"What happened then?" Evelyn looked at Cat, head tilted to the side.

Cat's eyes widened as she began to talk with her hands, vibrant in a way Zahara didn't often see from her quieter friend.

"Get this! The local Bedouin women defeated the Turks in 1917 in a local revolt. It was because of them some people think they ended up winning in the end. They managed to divert enough of the Ottomans' military resources that they couldn't beat the Brits."

Evelyn arched her eyebrow when Cat paused for air. "Did you memorize a textbook or something?"

Cat flushed, turning almost as red as her hair. "No...well, not exactly. I snuck a Petra tourist guide to read which I may or may not have finished on the drive over."

Zahara pursed her lips. "Ah, so the truth comes out. I wondered what you were so absorbed with reading when you weren't busy napping. It also explains why you kept randomly blurting out small factoids of info on the drive. It's fine—I'm glad at least one of us knows something. Where should we start, oh resident expert?"

Cat's color receded and she became animated again. "Let's go look at the bigger, more touristy stuff first. The place you're looking for probably isn't around there but this way, we can get to know the area before we get to the nuts and bolts of where we might find something pertaining to your family. I think it's important to get our bearings."

"And from there, we can spread out to other areas we may not be able to find otherwise." Evelyn grabbed her backpack.

"Sounds good to me. Lead on!" Zahara gestured at Cat, who flashed a smile along with a snappy salute as the three girls descended the hill from the parking lot into the valley.

Zahara was not disappointed. Petra was breathtaking and it felt like they were walking into history. The crumbling but still beautiful carved facades were etched into the rocks themselves, and even with the people milling about in modern dress, it was easy to transport herself to what it had been like back then.

Cat led them to the place known as *Al-Khazneh*, The Treasury, first. Of all the vague impressions she'd had of Petra, none lived up to how much more breathtaking it was to see in person. Even in the *Indiana Jones* movie, Hollywood hadn't come close to touching how magical it was. It seemed to almost hum with the promise of power. When they went to look at the equally impressive *Ad Deir*, called The Monastery in English, Zahara couldn't get over the disparity between the ornate and massive façades and the small, cave-like interiors they hid.

Breaking for a snack outside the Monastery, they watched as tourists poured in and out of the buildings. It had been quieter and chilly when Omar had dropped them off, but as the day wore on, it had become warm enough for Zahara to take her coat off. She left her scarf on to protect her neck from the breeze, but had allowed it to fall off her head as she grabbed one of the sandwiches he'd packed.

"Did you see anything, Cat?"

Cat shook her head. "No, nothing stands out. No auras except those of the tourists, who were all pretty normal. Actually, come to think of it, that seems a little strange in a place with this much history. Evelyn? Did you get anything?"

Zahara bit the inside of her cheek, remembering the way Evelyn had disappeared when she'd taken her to visit the cemetery in Edinburgh. She still felt bad about what had happened there, none of them realizing at the time Evelyn was able to see ghosts.

To her relief, Evelyn appeared unbothered as she took a bite of sandwich, chewed thoughtfully, then shook her head. "Nope. No spirits or residual energy so far as I can tell. Not like I'm disappointed about that. I do, however, agree it's strange. When I was in the graveyard with you guys, I was practically bombarded."

Cat frowned. "Some of the caves we saw were actual tombs, so you should have seen something."

"It's almost like the place has been wiped clean of whatever magic it had," Zahara murmured. It was strange. While the place was amazing and they'd had a great time hiking up and down the sides of the hilly valley in and out of caves, she was no closer to an answer about what to do with the amulet.

"Now what? I'm kind of out of ideas." Cat held up the tourist book and waved it at them. "We've been to all the major places. And it's almost five now. We're supposed to head back to the treasury to meet Omar."

Zahara sighed. "Well, we haven't been to the 'place of learning' yet, have we?"

Cat shrugged. "I'm not sure. They mention a place called the library, but it sounds like it's a tomb, not an actual library. We can go there before we head back to the treasury, if you want. It's on the way."

Zahara nodded then tried to choke down what remained of her sandwich.

This is it.

So far, the trip had been eerily normal, without a hint of supernatural anywhere. They hadn't come across any threats or signs of magic anywhere and that worried her more than actually coming across the jinn who'd been giving her nightmares all week.

She had the same back of the neck, prickly sensation she got when she watched a scary movie and the main character was about to do something stupid, like going into a basement alone.

Except in this case, the scary part wasn't obvious and it was the anticipation that was killing her.

As soon as they finished eating, they packed up what was left of their lunch and headed in the direction of the place Cat thought was the 'place of learning'. They weren't sure if that's what the letter from Reema meant, but it seemed a good place to check out before they met up with Omar.

But when they arrived at the tomb, Zahara was disappointed to see it was the same as all the others—another pretty facade with nothing more than rough-hewn stone cave walls on the inside. As they walked around beneath the seven-foot high ceiling in a room barely larger than the average coat room, Zahara fumed.

"This isn't right. None of this is right!" She rubbed her face with exasperation, wishing she could wipe off the irritation building up and giving her heartburn.

Cat wrinkled her nose. "I'm sorry, Zahara. It seemed promising. Don't forget we can always come back tomorrow. We should look through the smaller caves. I'm sure it's here somewhere. Even Robin said Petra was where the amulet needed to go, right?"

Zahara shook her head, gesturing around the room with her arm. "Well, it doesn't go here. In fact, this whole decrepit place hasn't got a hint of magic in it anywhere. I can feel more magic in downtown Edinburgh on High Street during rush hour than I'm getting from this entire dead city. Something is wrong."

She stopped abruptly. Something in her irritated outburst made her feel uneasy, but she wasn't sure which part. Was it her anger, or something she'd said? The dead city? Or the lack of magic?

As she looked around, more calmly this time, she realized it was true; there was nothing here except dirt and the fancy carvings of a lost civilization.

Evelyn nodded. "I think you're right, Zahara."

Her eyebrows went up. "About the magic? Or that the amulet doesn't go here?"

Evelyn's lip curled slightly. "Both about the magic and that it does but doesn't go here." When Zahara glared at her, she clarified. "I've seen this place in my dreams. So I agree with Cat when she says the necklace belongs here, but I also agree with you about the magic. It feels like something has been hidden. Kind of like if someone put a blanket over it and has damped it down so it can't be felt even by someone who is sensitive."

Zahara began to walk around the cave, trailing a hand along the wall as she inspected every nook and cranny. "You've hit the nail on the head." She turned to look at her friends again. "I think it's why this is bothering me so much. I'm feeling the anticipation and anxiety, but everything around us is flat and normal. I'm on edge because nothing is happening."

Cat agreed. "Like the calm before the storm."

"Exactly." Zahara sighed and pulled out the amulet from her bag.

It looked exactly the same as it had every other time she'd examined it. Feeling let down once more, she began to put it in her bag but just before she did, Cat gasped and pointed to the emerald.

"Look!"

Zahara hadn't noticed it at first. She'd been holding the necklace emerald-side down as she went to put it away, but now she could see the area beneath the stone was lighter and had begun glowing a faint green. As she watched, the light grew stronger. In fact, it was becoming so bright it reminded her of the Green Lantern's ring.

When she turned it over, the green seemed to be pulsing and was as bright as a torch. Her backpack fell forgotten to the ground with a faint plop she hardly registered. Cat and Evelyn approached with cautious expressions.

"Okay, that isn't normal." Evelyn pursed her lips and drew back slightly.

Zahara watched as Cat reached out and lightly brushed the surface of the emerald with her finger. She looked up with startled, wide eyes.

"It's warm!"

Zahara couldn't even nod in agreement as the rock began to pulse with heat. Something was definitely happening. A sudden need to put the necklace on filled her. Without questioning her motivation or the timing, Zahara slipped it over her head.

The warmth radiating from the emerald filled her chest and expanded the feeling of destiny that had begun to tickle at her consciousness the second she'd seen the stone light up.

"Um, are you sure you should be doing that?" Evelyn's worried expression caught her eye.

Zahara put a hand on the necklace and was about to answer when her friend's features began to blur. Warmth and green light overpowered her as the eerie green fog filled her vision. The sound of someone screaming made her look around but all she could see was green light everywhere.

Then everything became still.

CHAPTER 9

Zahara blinked, finally able to open her eyes when the blinding green light faded. She was surprised to see she was still in the same cave she'd been in a split second earlier. Everything was exactly the same, except her friends were missing.

Her heart rate sped up as she looked around, unable to see them or her backpack. The only thing other than rocks and sand in the cave was her. Biting her lip, she forced herself to walk to the mouth of the cave. Once there, she sat down with a thump, shaking her head.

"This isn't happening. I'm unconscious or something. Maybe it's a dream."

Gone were the tourists who had been swarming around earlier. Gone were the signs advertising food and beverages. She couldn't even see the parking lot. If she had to make a wild guess, she'd say she was in an alternate version of Petra.

Or an alternate time. *Was it possible?*

She looked at the amulet around her neck. It wasn't a dream. Wherever she was, whatever was happening, it had done this to her.

The necklace twinkled up at her in the late afternoon sunshine, looking innocent and unchanged from when she'd first seen it fall out of the envelope into her surprised hands at her parents' house.

She stared back into the empty cave. "Now what?"

As if an answer to her question, a faint noise caught her attention from somewhere nearby. She scooted to the side of the cave entrance and hid behind a pillar. Walking beside a camel loaded with colorful parcels about twenty feet away from her was a woman.

Zahara hesitated. Should she try to speak with her, or was the woman someone she was supposed to avoid? Before she could make up her mind, the decision was taken out of her hands.

As though able to smell her, the stranger raised her head from the path and paused, looking all around until she stopped, her head cocked in the direction where Zahara was hiding.

Pulling back behind the rock with a racing heart, she took a deep breath. "Maybe she can tell you where you are. You can do this."

As pep talks went, Zahara had little to work with. The woman appeared normal but after fighting soulless people in the past, she knew looks could be deceiving until you got close enough to see the whites of their eyes. Or lack thereof. Without any better options, she stepped forward from the mouth of the cave and let the woman see her.

"Hello?" Zahara said, then realized the woman probably didn't speak English. Her Arabic was poor, but hopefully what she knew would be enough to ask a few questions. "*Marhabaan*?"

The woman's head snapped up, and their eyes met. Hers were wide and curious, with a warmth that somehow made Zahara feel welcome. They crinkled into a smile as she left her camel where it was and approached Zahara.

"*Marhabaan.* I see you have come on a long journey."

Zahara nodded, watching her cautiously. She looked nice, unthreatening. Her hair was covered modestly and she appeared to be in her early twenties. At the warmth in the stranger's face, some of her anxiety faded, but not all.

"Yes. I have. I was sent by my family on a journey to return something very important."

Without thinking of discretion or anything else, Zahara began to lift the amulet out of her shirt to tell the stranger everything, but the woman held up a hand with an alarmed expression.

"No! Not here. Follow me. This is a place where the stones have ears and the sand has memory. We can go somewhere safer and talk, but best to keep your story to only those you mean to tell."

Zahara let the amulet drop. *Why did I do that?* She knew better than to tell a stranger anything on a good day, let alone now. Yet something about this woman made her feel they were destined to meet and it was completely okay to tell her everything.

She didn't believe in coincidences. With one last look at the empty cave, she accepted that her bag and friends were really gone and she was alone. Perhaps the woman in front of her was her best shot at making it home.

Taking a deep breath, she followed the stranger into the bright desert day.

THEY PLODDED ALONG beside the camel for about twenty minutes. Around the time Zahara was beginning to feel parched, the woman gestured to a crack in the rocks. From where Zahara stood, it was almost completely hidden, and she was certain she wouldn't have noticed it on her own.

"Here. We go through this *siq*. On the other side it is safer. We can talk there."

Zahara's palms began to sweat as she followed, and she cast a last look back to where they'd come from. She wondered if she was heading into an ambush and found herself clenching her hands into sweaty fists, just in case.

She was relieved when the pass widened as they walked through it, and when she looked up, awe replaced her trepidation. The wall extended several stories above her head. It had been worn smooth by wind, or maybe water, which gave it the appearance of a smooth, cleanly etched swoop. This continued for another few minutes until it abruptly gave way to a lush, green oasis.

"This is beautiful!"

Zahara breathed out, and when she inhaled again, the familiar tingle of magic washed over her. It was like a refreshing shower after the lack she'd experienced within Petra itself. She hadn't realized how cut off she'd felt until the magic had come rushing back.

The woman looked at her and smiled. "Ah, I see. You noticed the absence earlier, didn't you? What is your nature?"

The question was without artifice or guile. Once again, Zahara felt strangely comfortable answering her true meaning without hesitation.

"Earth."

She waited for the woman to reply, wondering what kind of person she was to be able to ask a stranger such a difficult yet deceptively simple question.

The woman nodded. "Then things must have been very difficult for you in Petra. Of course you noticed it is a dead place. All of the magic disappeared long ago. Stolen."

Zahara was perplexed. "How is that possible? I've never been anywhere without magic. Even in the largest of cities, I can feel some, trapped beneath the buildings."

The woman's forehead wrinkled then smoothed out. "You must indeed be from far away if you do not know this. There was an earthquake, caused by a great battle between two rival jinns. It is said they leached out all the magic during their Great War, and this is the reason Petra fell."

Zahara nodded. That would explain why the place had felt so dead to them as they walked around. Evelyn had commented on how even the expected ghosts hadn't been evident.

"But how could they have removed all the magic if the earth remains? Wouldn't it regenerate in time, or cause the entire area to collapse without it?"

The woman shrugged. "It is something I have never wondered about. Maybe it will, maybe it will not. It is what it is at this moment, right now. There is no use wishing for things to be any other way than what they are."

After her philosophical and somewhat circular reply, she turned and walked toward a wall that bent to the right. Zahara followed, more curious now than she'd been earlier now that some of her fear had been replaced by questions. Hopefully, the woman had some answers.

After they passed through the bend in the wall, she saw a small tent beside a fenced garden plot. A clear pond, large enough to serve as a water source was a few feet away from it, and chickens pecked the ground nearby. The sound of a baby crying broke the silence of the quaint scene and the woman's pace picked up.

A baby?

Following with a shade more reluctance after hearing the crying, she entered a few steps behind the woman into the home. It was similar to the tent they'd slept in the first night after they'd arrived in the desert, except this one gave her an overwhelming sense of coziness. With pillows and blankets in one corner, which appeared to be a lounging area, and a small kitchen in front of them, it felt like a home.

An older woman stood in the kitchen, making shushing noises at a baby with tears rolling down its chubby cheeks. The woman scurried forward and scooped the child out of the old woman's arms, crooning softly to it before looking at Zahara again.

"Please, come in. Take your shoes off at the door. Would you like some coffee?" She continued to croon and sway until the baby broke into a smile.

Zahara didn't want to impose, especially now that she knew the woman had a child to look after. "Only if it is no trouble."

To her surprise, her guide addressed the old woman in response. "*Umi*, this woman has been traveling for days. Look how thin her face is! Can you make her a coffee and some food? She looks like she could use some."

Zahara touched her cheek with a frown. She wasn't that thin, but compared to the round cheeks of the other women in the tent, she did feel a little gaunt. The older woman nodded with a shy smile then turned her back and began to prepare a plate of food in the small kitchen. Moments later, she placed it on the low table beside the cushions, gesturing for her to sit down.

"Thank you." Zahara bowed her head as she sat, taking a careful sip of the coffee. Her eyes widened. "It's sweet!"

The older woman smiled, her wrinkles arranging themselves into lines of joy. "Turkish style."

Zahara took another sip, savoring the flavor. It reminded her in some ways of the Starbuck's sweetness of their fancy coffees except for the way it boldly retained the sharp taste of coffee.

"Now that we are safer, we can speak of your journey. What is your name?"

The young woman who had led Zahara to her home without any qualms now sat across from her, holding the baby as she watched with her head tilted to the side.

"My name is Zahara Khan. I'm from Scotland, but my ancestors are from around here somewhere. I came to return this amulet to somewhere called 'the place of learning'. Somehow, I ended up here instead." Zahara held up the necklace she was wearing for the woman to see.

The woman examined it carefully before turning to her mother. They shared a look Zahara didn't understand before she finally sighed. "I had a feeling you were important. I do not know of this Scotland, but that is a powerful necklace. I know of it, and that it has been missing for hundreds of years, maybe longer. Where did you get it?"

Zahara shrugged before letting the amulet fall back to rest on her chest. It was oddly comfortable now, like it belonged on her body.

"It came in the mail. A distant relative died recently and sent it to me. I didn't know her, but she left me a note saying she wanted me to bring it back here, to Petra. I wish I knew where I was supposed to leave it or why it was so important, but I'm basically taking everything on faith."

"This necklace has a powerful magic. It can hold the shape of many spells inside it, including one said to be able to transport the wearer to other times and places."

The woman suddenly covered her face with a hand before dropping it to reveal a sheepish smile. Wondering if her action had something to do with the necklace, Zahara did not expect what she heard next.

"Forgive me. I have neglected introductions. You have been most gracious to trust me without even knowing my name! I am Reema, and this is my mother, and my son, Haytham."

CHAPTER 10

Zahara nearly choked on her coffee. "I'm sorry. Did you say your name is Reema?"

She searched the woman's face, wishing she knew what her relative had looked like. It had to be a coincidence. It wasn't like it was an uncommon Arabic name. But what were the chances there was no connection given everything else?

Was she supposed to give this Reema the necklace?

She nodded. "Yes, I did. You say you are from Scotland? We are travelers as well and have only been in this area for a few months. We fled from my home, my *umi*, husband, and I, when it was no longer safe for us to stay there. The peace in this hidden valley has been good with a baby to care for."

Reema paused, blinking rapidly, and Zahara wondered if she should pat her shoulder. She settled for platitudes instead.

"I'm sorry to hear that."

Reema quickly regained control and smiled down at the now-cooing baby. "Thank you. It was a difficult time, but it has been worth it to see my child so happy here."

Zahara could see the love in her eyes and for the first time, she wondered what it would be like to have a child of her own. It was hard to imagine she would ever be able to sleep worrying about something happening to them with all the danger she'd already dealt with.

"Why did you leave your home? Why wasn't it safe there?"

Reema looked up, her face now drawn and tired, as if re-living the memory. "My husband is a powerful man, a jinn, but even with his powers we had to leave the court of Suleyman for our own protection. We chose to settle here, because it is a place of little magic. Hopefully, our enemy will pass us without notice if he ever happens by this little shelter."

Something she'd said bothered Zahara. "Wait, did you say...Suleyman? Like, the Magnificent?"

She shrugged. "I'm not sure how magnificent he is, but he rules the Ottoman Empire, which stretches across the desert to the seas. Some may call him great, but I would say if he is, it is because of the advisors he has surrounded himself. My husband was one of his most important at the court, at least he was until he met me."

Zahara gulped. She didn't know what year it was, but she'd listened to Cat long enough to recognize the name Suleyman. She may be in Petra, but it was definitely not the same one she'd started off in. Somehow, the green light from the amulet had thrown her back in time.

Way, way back in time.

She tried to calm herself by taking a deep breath. Stay calm. You just need to figure this out."Why did he leave court if he was so powerful?"

Maybe if I can get more information, I can find a way to get home. The necklace brought me here for some reason. I just have to figure out why.

Reema gazed down at Haytham, stroking his cheek with one gentle finger before looking at Zahara with determination. "He left it behind for love. Together we have made our own empire. It may be a small one, but it is all we could ever desire, the gift of being a family together with our son. He is the reason we must remain hidden."

Zahara nodded. "He's a beautiful child. But why did you have to leave? Couldn't you have stayed at court with a baby?"

Reema smiled sadly as her voice dropped to a whisper. "My husband was promised to the daughter of a powerful jinn at the time he came to prominence in court. When she was of age, he was expected to marry her. All was proceeding according to plan until the day my husband saw me in the marketplace. That was it. We fell instantly in love and knew we couldn't bear to be apart. So we made plans. He tried to get out of his promise honorably, but the other jinn refused to accept any of his offerings."

Her voice broke and this time Zahara leaned over and did place a hand on her shoulder. She wished she could do more, but clearly, this was a difficult memory. "I'm so sorry. You don't have to continue—it really isn't any of my business."

Reema's lip curled slightly as she shook her head. "It is okay. I have had no companions other than my love and my *umi*, so it is nice to get it out. It is always easier to lighten one's burden by sharing the load."

Zahara met her smile with one of her own. "In that case, I would like to know everything you wish to share."

Reema looked at her son. He'd fallen asleep and she kissed him on the forehead before she continued. "This jinn was older and far more powerful than my love. He lacked any compassion for others, and we knew that if we stayed, he would never rest until he had destroyed my husband and killed me, regardless of the baby."

Her eyes hardened. In that instant, Zahara saw the scared woman turn into a warrior in front of her.

"For my husband and son, I would do anything. We ran away together as soon as I found out I was with child. Most of my family didn't approve. Jinns are not seen as trustworthy in most circumstances, not to mention the shame I brought to my family by my condition."

Zahara's eyes widened as understanding sank in. "Oh, um. I'm assuming you hadn't already gotten married?"

Reema blushed, briefly looking away to hide her pink cheeks. "Not at first. But before I left, my *umi* helped me sneak away. We said our vows in secret, then traveled day and night until we reached this place. While the majority of Petra is bereft of magic, this hidden pocket of earth magic made it possible for us to stay here in relative comfort."

Zahara could see how much Reema loved her little family and her heart twisted as she watched the mother and child together. She would love to have her own one day, hopefully under better circumstances. She looked around the tent, a sudden curiosity about where Reema's husband was filling her as she realized there was no sign of him anywhere.

Gesturing around herself, Zahara hoped she wasn't being rude. "Where is your husband now?"

She regretted the question immediately when her host's face drained of color.

"He is missing. He left to get supplies two days ago and was only going as far as Wadi Musa. He should have been back already. That is the reason why I was out searching the path when I came across you. I'd already been away from Haytham long enough and I was on my way home when we met. I hope he is okay, but I have no way to know for sure and can now do nothing but wait. I decided to bring you with me because you seemed so lost. I know what that feels like."

Zahara grimaced. She wasn't sure how far Wadi Musa was by foot, but remembered Omar saying it was only a few minutes by car. Even factoring in the extra time it would take a person carrying supplies to walk, it shouldn't take longer than a day to get there and back.

"Is there anything I can do to help?"

She felt bad for this young mother. The man she'd left everything for was missing and she must be frightened he wouldn't come back, given the way they'd had to leave. It must be overwhelming. To be alone except for her mum and baby while she waited.

Her eyes fell on the sleeping baby. Objectively he was adorable, with a little button nose and big brown eyes. They'd been full of tears when she'd first seen them but they were closed now. In sleep, he had long eyelashes that brushed his cheeks. His tiny lips blew small bubbles, which made him almost more endearing than she could bear. She didn't know how old he was but thought maybe about a year.

Reema sighed, bringing Zahara's attention back to her.

"Thank you for your offer, but I'm not sure what *I* should be doing. At this time there is nothing you can do except keep me company, which you are already doing a wonderful job with. He has gone before but has always been back within a day, unless weather caused a delay. He's never been gone for this long, and I am worried our hiding place has been found. If that is the case, my child is in danger."

She squeezed the infant tighter, causing him to squirm in his sleep and let out a small squeak of protest.

"Shhhh, *habibi*, shhhh." She wrinkled her nose, smiling sadly at Zahara. "I squeezed too hard in my distress. He enjoys a tight embrace, but not so tight." She stood up, swaying him from side to side until he settled again. "As I was saying, he's never been this late. It is not a good sign. I feel we should be prepared for an attack but I have only a small gift of earth magic, barely enough for growing vegetables. My love renewed his protections on our home before he left. Hopefully, it will be enough."

Reema was still swaying with the baby but stopped moving to stare at the tent entrance as she worried her lip with small, white teeth.

Zahara wasn't sure what she could do to protect them with her fox form, but she had become more proficient at using her magic defensively when she'd battled against the hordes of soulless with her friends the year before. And if her magic wasn't enough, she also had her stubbornness. According to her brothers, that was a weapon all by itself.

"I think I can help you."

"Thank you. I will accept your offer, but I'm not sure what to tell you to do just yet."

"We should cast a protection spell."

Zahara jumped, startled to hear Reema's mum speak for the first time. She'd remained nearby but Zahara had forgotten about her. Clearly, she'd been listening closely even though she hadn't contributed to the conversation until now.

Reema's eyes widened. "What kind of spell, *Umi*?"

The old woman shrugged, her face falling. "I am not sure. Perhaps Marwan has some books?"

Reema looked as though a light bulb had gone off. Passing the sleeping child to her mum, she went over to a large trunk in the far corner of the room. Unfastening an ornate bronze clasp, she drew a thick book out from deep inside. Closing the trunk and hefting the book onto her hip, she walked back and carefully placed it on the table.

"Marwan showed me this book once. He said it was very special and important. He told me that if I ever needed anything when he wasn't around to help I should look in here first. Thank you, *Umi*. I had forgotten about his words until you reminded me."

Zahara stared at the book on the table. It reminded her of an old family bible she'd seen once, in the library at the university while waiting for Cat. While not much of a historian herself, she could tell the book was ancient, which in turn made her wonder how old it really was. If she remembered the dates Cat had been spouting from her guidebook earlier, she was pretty sure the amulet had someone brought her back to the 1500s, and the book in front of her was already at least one hundred years old or more.

"May I?"

She held her hand out to touch it and when Reema nodded, she moved closer to examine it in detail. It was a deep emerald green, covered with shapes and letters that swirled on the cover. As she watched, they seemed to be rearranging themselves, shaping words or pictures before reforming into other words or shapes. Some were familiar to her, like the sun and stars. Others were completely indecipherable.

The moment her hand made contact with the cover it began to give off a soft green glow, the same glow the amulet had produced right before she'd wound up in the past. Her hand jerked away at the memory and she looked back at Reema uncertainly.

"I think the amulet and the book are connected. The amulet did that for me as well."

Reema's eyes widened and she crowded closer to watch. "What does it say?"

The sweet smell of baby filled Zahara's nose and instantly some of her fear departed, giving her the strength to touch it again. This time, the glow remained muted. When it didn't immediately whisk her away, she took a deep breath and opened it. After turning the first page, she stopped.

"My Arabic isn't good enough to read this. I'm sorry." She passed back the book, irritated to be so close and yet unable to understand the words.

Reema shook her head. "It is better than mine. I cannot read at all."

Zahara was floored. She'd never met someone who couldn't read before. She'd totally forgotten that up until the last few decades, many people around the world never learned to read at all.

What she took for granted was a privilege in some places, even now.

Frustration burned inside her chest and Zahara rubbed a hand against her sternum, as if the movement would make it go away. "So what can we do?"

She could probably piece together the words, but it would take time. Not to mention a chance of blowing them all up, or worse, if they did a spell incorrectly. All it would take was misinterpreting a word or reversing the order of a crucial step.

She waited as Reema and her *umi* looked at each other then back at her. Their faces were downcast, reflecting her own pessimistic thoughts. Suddenly tired of her own negative thinking, she inhaled and took the book back. Instead of whining, she could at least try before quitting.

Praying that her grade three level Arabic would be enough to comprehend a spell book written in a medieval, Middle Eastern dialect, she leaned over to read. A gust of wind blew through the tent, extinguishing the lights.

Her heart stopped.

CHAPTER 11

At first, everything was dark. Once her mind caught up with her terror, Zahara was able to see the sun was still shining outside. Slivers of light came through the tent, and when her eyes adjusted to the dimness, it was enough for her to see the tense faces of Reema and her mum looking at the entrance.

Reema moved swiftly with silent grace, placing the sleeping Haytham into a small nest of blankets where he didn't stir or make a noise. Once he was settled, she zipped across the room and replaced the book in the trunk before huddling closer to Zahara and her *umi*.

"What should we do? Should we hide?"

Zahara kept her voice to a whisper, hoping if there was someone outside they wouldn't hear her. She couldn't handle the idea of sitting frozen like a mouse in front of a predator. She needed to do something.

She may be small, but she was a fox after all. She preferred running and attacking rather than waiting for danger to strike.

Reema hid her face in her hands, the shimmer of fear in her eyes blotted out by slim hands. "I do not know what to do. I am hopeful it is Marwan, but it may not be."

Zahara stood up. Seeing the two women scared had begun to make her angry. That was it—she was done waiting. "I'm going to take a look. Don't be alarmed, I'll shift into my earth shape to check it out."

Zahara didn't wait to see how the two women would take the transformation. As she let the tingle sweep through her, everything within her body relaxed. She was always more comfortable as the small desert fox. Once she was done, she slunk toward the entrance of the tent, nearly invisible in the pale light. She had just reached her target when the tent door swirled open on the heels of another gust of wind, revealing a tall figure standing silhouetted in the doorway.

His clothing was as dark as his hair, and when his eyes flashed deep green in the muted light, her heart leapt into her throat. Was he the jinn after Reema? Her eyes flicked to the young woman, but when she saw relief and joy flood her face, she knew everything was okay even before she moved.

Reema rushed to the man and launched into his arms. "Marwan!"

He caught her, holding Reema tightly against him for a moment before grasping her shoulders and drawing back so slowly it was easy to tell he didn't want to let go of her either. He was breathing hard, and while he appeared happy to see Reema, his face was drawn and his clothing was stained with dirt as well as something that looked and smelled suspiciously like blood. She knew he wasn't here for a happy reunion with his family.

Danger had found him, after all.

"We must pack, *habibi*. It is no longer safe for us here. Grab what you need. Quickly. We do not have much time." His words were spoken in between gasps of air, urgent and clipped.

How much of the way he spoke was from the circumstances she wasn't sure, but he looked like he'd ran all the way back. Zahara's fox brain told her to stay crouched down, warning her insistently that things weren't safe even before Marwan had said it out loud.

Slinking closer to the tent's entrance to try to see outside, she didn't like what she saw. It had been sunny earlier, but now the sky was a threatening dark grey. It looked as though the heavens were about to open up and storm, and she crept back, not eager to be soaked.

She looked up into the face of the jinn before her and suddenly knew. This man was her great, great, great, however many times removed, grandfather. As close as she was to him, she recognized his features as well as she knew her own name. He had the same dimples as her brother Sufiyan, but his jaw was a replica of her grandfather's.

His eyes, on the other hand, glowed with a power unlike anyone in her family. The glow was identical to the dark green light which had risen from the amulet and the book when she'd touched them. She remained tucked behind the leg of a chair, motionless as Reema was deposited carefully on the floor beside her, at which point his eyes moved to her with a laser-like focus.

"Ah." Without letting go of Reema, he examined her and nodded once. "I see the visitor I've been expecting has arrived. Good."

Reema pulled back, wrinkling her forehead. "You expected Zahara?"

He looked down, his expression enigmatic. "Yes. It was foreseen. She is needed for the spell to succeed. For us to defeat Abbas and live free of reprisal."

"You never said anything. I thought after all this time we were safe. I had hoped...maybe he'd forgotten."

Marwan reached down, stroking her cheek. "Abbas doesn't forget, *habibi*. He will search for us until the sun falls from the sky. Until the moon and stars no longer light the way for the caravans. We now have all the pieces we need for the spell to cast him away from us for eternity. In order to keep our children, and our children's children, free from his evil presence, we must complete it before he finds us."

Zahara crept forward as he spoke, her curiosity outweighing any hesitation at his words.

Marwan caught the movement and smiled. "It is a pleasure to meet you, Zahara Khan. Thank you for coming. You have brought the amulet with you, yes?"

She nodded and felt her fox head bobbing. Realizing she was out of place, she transformed back in to her human shape. "Yes, I did. I don't understand how or why I had to bring it though. Shouldn't it have been available for you to cast the original spell? If I was alive and well in the 21st century, doesn't that mean the spell was already completed?"

He gave her a mysterious smile as his green eyes darkened.

"Time is a funny thing, little fox. The amulet does not belong to one point in time only, but can go where and when it is needed. It is tied to the spell book you have no doubt already seen, however, and has chosen to reappear for us now because it is time. All the elements necessary for us to succeed are together at last. We must cast this spell before Abbas arrives to rid ourselves of him forever and protect our descendants from his cruel retribution."

Zahara still didn't understand completely but nodded anyway. *Whatever. As long as this works and I get to go home.*

Holding the amulet up, she felt the glow before she saw it. She took it off like it was hot, remembering the episode in the cave and frightened what would happen next. She offered it to Marwan, but he shook his head and folded his hands together.

"Um, okay then. What do we need to do?"

"It is not for me to wield. You and Reema must do this together. It is vitally important to provide the power for the spell. Reema, you remember the spell book I showed you?"

She rushed across the room to the place she'd hidden the book and retrieved it, carrying the heavy tome back to Marwan. With a sigh of relief, he placed it on the table, glancing over his shoulder at Zahara.

"We must begin. I only narrowly escaped Abbas's minions. They caught me on the road, and while I managed to dispatch them, they won't stay away for long."

He flipped through the pages, eventually stopping on one with a combination of intricate drawings and ornately etched words and tapped at the page.

"This is the page you require. It is a permanent binding spell. If you are able to cast it correctly, it will hold the subject for a million years in the in-between. If you cast it incorrectly, it will trap you in the same place instead. To avoid that circumstance, you must follow the instructions perfectly."

A lump stuck in her throat but Zahara managed to choke it down far enough to ask about the obvious omission. "You said 'you'. You're not going to help?"

Marwan shook his head. "I cannot. Abbas draws nearer even as we speak. I must leave shortly to protect my family. Reema; you, Zahara, and your *umi* can do this together. Protect Haytham with your life. Always remember how much I love you."

Reema began to cry silently, but Zahara saw the power in her face through the tears. Her heart may have been breaking, but her chin was set with determination.

"I will protect our son with my last breath. Please be safe. Come back to me. I cannot live without you."

Marwan turned away from the book and moved closer to her. As he swept her into a passionate embrace, Zahara turned her head to give them privacy. Her eyes fell on their sleeping son. The depth of the love she could feel between them was something she couldn't understand.

What would I be willing to endure for love?

She gave them their moment; knowing with a sudden, sharp wrench in her chest it may be the last one they ever shared.

A loud bang came from the crevice outside the tent, followed immediately by the low rumble of falling rocks. It sounded as if a bomb had gone off. She stumbled when the earth shook but caught herself in time to avoid hitting the ground.

Dust floated in the entrance of the tent, sparkling in the weak sunlight.

"He's here."

Marwan gave Reema one last kiss and met her eyes with a look of love and sadness so intense it broke Zahara's heart. Then, as soon as it had begun, it ended. He moved toward the door, pausing to look at the baby with a bittersweet smile.

"Tell my son I love him and I'm proud of him. Raise him to be a strong, kind man. I love you. Until we meet again, *habibata*."

Zahara watched him leave. As the flap of the tent opened, she caught a glimpse of the damage outside. The thought this would be the last time she saw him settled into her bones, and she turned to find Reema had likely had the same thought. She had collapsed onto the rug, shoulders trembling as she sobbed.

Suppressing her own sadness for the couple, she shook Reema's shoulders gently. "Reema, you must get up. There is no time. We have to start the spell. If we can finish it before Abbas arrives, maybe we can stop him and Marwan will return without injury."

Reema wailed with despair. "It's hopeless! You said yourself you can't read in Arabic and I can't read at all. How are we supposed to complete the spell without destroying ourselves?"

Zahara shrugged. "Hey, I'm still not entirely sure how I got here in the first place. All I know is that it had something to do with this necklace and it suddenly be able to glow. This is bigger than you or me and involves many generations, if your husband is right. One thing I know from being in other situations out of my control is that events are going to continue to unfold no matter how I feel about them. Basically, what I'm trying to say is that if I can travel hundreds of years through time and not explode or disintegrate or whatever, I'm betting my reading skills will somehow end up being good enough."

Reema met her eyes. Her face was streaked with dust and tears but she looked a little more hopeful.

Zahara squeezed her shoulder. "Come on. That last explosion sounded like it was on the path we used to get here. I saw rubble where the crevice hides this place, and I'm worried Abbas is trying to trap us here so he can come for you after..."

Zahara stopped talking when Reema's face paled further.

"Trap us? What should we do?"

"We cast the spell. You need to get up. I know you're upset right now—" Zahara hastily qualified her statement when Reema's face became indignant. "More than upset. Justifiably so. But we need to move."

Reema dashed the tears off her cheeks and pushed herself up to her feet, setting her chin the same way Zahara had seen her do earlier when she'd promised to keep her son safe. With that one small gesture, Zahara knew her stubbornness was genetic.

"You are right. I must protect Haytham. This spell gives us a way to do that. I would walk across hell and back to make sure he stays safe. For those I love, I will attempt anything."

Impressed at her strength, Zahara turned to the book and began to read.

CHAPTER 12

C at and Evelyn stood in the cave, silent as the stone around them as they looked around in a state of shock.

"What the what was that?" Cat blinked around at the otherwise empty cave.

Evelyn's eyes were wide. "I have no clue. One minute we were searching corners for anything remotely magical, the next thing I knew, Zahara's necklace was glowing like it was the freakin' Aurora Borealis. Please tell me I didn't hallucinate her disappearance—or better yet, tell me I did."

The sound of her screams still seemed to reverberate in the small cave as they stared at the spot where Zahara had been. One minute she'd been beside them, then, in a flash of green light, she'd vanished along with the necklace. Her backpack lay on the floor of the cave as if forgotten; a silent witness she'd once stood there. But there was no sign of their friend anywhere.

Cat's hand flew to her mouth. "The necklace!"

Evelyn nodded, picking up the bag. "Yup. That was super weird."

Cat watched her concentrate on the bag, knowing she was trying to get an image of Zahara. But when she opened her eyes and shook her head grimly, Cat jogged over to the mouth of the cave and halted at the entrance, straining to see around the exterior.

"Maybe she's outside, waiting for us. It probably got too creepy in here with the glowing. That's possible, right? It could have happened."

Evelyn threw the bag over her shoulder and joined Cat, raising an eyebrow when she turned hopeful eyes to her. She laid a hand on her arm. "Do you really believe that?"

"No, I don't believe it." Cat's shoulders slumped as she kicked the dirt at her feet. "I was hoping it sounded more logical out loud than it did in my head. Zahara's gone, isn't she?"

Evelyn pressed her lips together and rubbed her forehead. "Appears so."

They looked around a while longer before Cat began to pace, hugging her arms to herself. "I still don't feel any magic here. How could this have happened? We need to find out where she went."

Evelyn intercepted her stiff movements with a hug, which Cat accepted, leaning into her shoulder. "Should we meet Omar as planned, or do you want to stay here and look around longer?"

Cat shook her head against Evelyn's shoulder then drew back, looking resigned. "Normally I'd say we should keep looking. Like, leave no man behind and all. But we were here. We saw her vanish. There's absolutely no way she got lost or kidnapped. She's not here. We both saw the amulet glowing with magic. Wherever she is, we're going to need all the help we can get to bring her back. I vote we find Omar now and fill him in on what happened. Maybe he'll know something."

Evelyn nodded. "And if not, at least he's from the area. Maybe one of his connections will know where she went and how to get her back. If that's the case, let's jet. He said he'd meet us at five and it's almost five now."

Cat nodded, blinking away tears as she took a deep breath. "Okay. Maybe you can have a chat with Robin too. This is way out of our usual face-to-face kind of fight, and I'm pretty sure wherever Zahara is now, she needs his help."

As they left the ancient cave, she threw one last look over her shoulder. "I hope we aren't making the wrong choice."

Evelyn gave her a commiserating look and slung an arm around her friend.

"I know."

BY THE TIME THEY ARRIVED at the meeting point near the treasury, the women were almost half an hour late. Omar was pacing back and forth, but when he saw them he stopped. His smile faded as he realized only two women were approaching, not three as he expected.

"Where is Zahara?" He looked behind Cat and Evelyn, praying he'd see her there, coming around the corner. But he already knew, deep down, she wasn't coming.

He'd been nervous to leave her in Petra with her friends, even though he'd had no good reason to feel that way. Part of him had feared she wouldn't be coming back to him today almost before he'd brought them.

It wasn't because Robin had said anything; he'd been irritatingly vague, even for him. That hadn't bothered him when they'd first spoken. He hadn't known the girls then, after all.

They were a job like any other. He'd known the basics and his plan had been the usual; pick them up, feed them, shelter them for a few nights, and get them to Petra and back in one piece.

Now he wished he'd asked a few more questions. Knowing Petra as well as he did, he'd been surprised they were heading there, but not alarmed. Merely curious why they'd want to go to such a well-known magical dead spot instead of anywhere else. They should have been completely safe, especially with a magical amulet like the one Zahara had been wearing.

But now...the absence of a girl he'd just met and barely knew pricked at him with a sense of loss disproportionate to how long they'd been aquainted. It was confusing and more troubling than he'd imagined.

"She just...vanished," said Cat.

When he looked at the pale redhead, he saw devastation etched onto her face. Before he could comment, his attention was drawn toward Evelyn, who was holding up the third back-pack with a frown.

"We saw a flash of green light from the amulet she was wearing, then she vanished. This was all she left behind."

Omar took the backpack, looking at it blankly for a few beats before he was able to shake himself out of his strange feeling of loss and back to the situation at hand. He started to speak but halted at the intensity of the look Cat was directing at Evelyn.

"We need to talk to Robin," Cat said

Evelyn sighed. "I know. I'll ask him."

Both women turned to him and he took a half-step back when Evelyn's dark eyes caught his. Something struck him as strange and he had to blink and look away.

Had her eyes been glowing? No, they couldn't be.

When he looked again, he saw merely the same pretty, tawny-beige face with deep brown eyes, not the swirling magical opals he thought he'd seen. He realized she was watching him, chin down and eyebrows raised, and a flush crept over his face.

Was I staring?

Once she had his attention, she waved an arm. "Is there a place nearby where we can gate to Robin?"

He shook his head, grateful for a question he could answer. "No, the only gate I can access is the one where I picked you up. The earthquake ages ago destroyed the one inside Petra. There is one a little closer than Saudi, but the area it's in makes it unsafe for us to attempt."

Evelyn nodded. "I was expecting you to say that. Okay, Cat. I'll have to ask him tonight."

Omar tilted his head, frowning. "You'll ask Robin tonight? I don't understand. It will take us too long to get to the gate to make that possible."

A ghost of a smile flickered on Cat's drawn face. "Her and Robin, they're kind of a thing."

Evelyn shrugged. "I found out not too long ago we go way, way back. I guess you could call him my boyfriend. I have the power to control dreams, so I can always contact him while I'm sleeping. We should go back to Amman, unless you've found something closer for tonight?"

He nodded, trying to process what she'd just told him. She was Robin's girlfriend? Lord Robin, Earth God of the British Isles, had a girlfriend? He frowned, feeling stupid and a little disappointed in himself. Why hadn't Robin said anything? It made sense now why he'd been so insistent about keeping these women safe.

"Yes, actually, I secured hotel rooms in Wadi Musa while you were exploring. It's a place I know well with a nice restaurant and very good prices." He looked back in the direction girls had come from. "You're sure Zahara isn't in the caves? Maybe we should look for her again."

Cat touched his shoulder lightly, causing a small tingle to travel into him, easing some of the knot in his stomach which Zahara's absence had created. His eyebrows drew together but relaxed at the look on her face.

"I'm sorry, Omar. She really did vanish. Neither of us can sense her in Petra anymore. If she was here, we would be able to feel it. I don't think we can find her where she is right now. Let Evelyn talk to Robin. Maybe he can help this time."

Omar sighed and turned his back to Petra. The place he'd last seen the woman who'd made his heart warm for the first time in a century. "If you are certain, we should go. The sooner Evelyn contacts Robin, the better."

AFTER A SHORT DRIVE, they checked in at the hotel then had a quiet supper. Cat and Evelyn rehashed the events in the cave for Omar, but it didn't help. He couldn't get his mind off Zahara's absence.

Where had she gone? Was she injured somewhere, all alone? Was she trapped and scared? He felt so helpless. He'd just found her and now he'd lost her before he had a chance to explore the strange way he was drawn to her. He prayed to Allah Evelyn would be able to get something useful from Robin for a change. He liked the god, but he'd always been unpredictable.

Once they had discussed everything in detail, conversation dried up like rain in the desert. They picked at their food without interest even though objectively, it tasted fine. When they'd had enough, he showed the girls to their room.

"I'll come back at seven to get you for breakfast." He looked at Evelyn, unable to keep the longing from his face. "I hope Robin can help."

Evelyn pressed her lips into a thin smile. "Me too. We'll talk in the morning. Hopefully, I'll have good news by then. Goodnight."

Omar waited until they closed the door before walking away. Different thoughts struggled for dominance but those of Zahara won out by the time he reached his room. He tried to relax and fall asleep, but her memory wouldn't leave him alone.

Finally, unable to still the restlessness, he gave up and went outside. Looking around to make sure he was alone, he found a secluded spot near some scrubby bushes and allowed himself to transform. Tingling all over, he shifted into the familiar red fur and darted off into the night.

OMAR ROLLED OVER IN bed with a groan as the sun broke through the shoddy hotel curtains. He'd slept in many hotels through the years, and he'd never been impressed with their attempt at curtains. None ever blocked the light, but maybe that was intentional to make sure there was no chance of sleeping in and missing check out time.

He stumbled to the shower, allowing the hot water to wash away the grime from his midnight run. He'd needed the exercise to sleep, but it hadn't done anything to stop him from thinking about Zahara. Her memory had joined him in his dreams after all.

He glanced at his watch and saw it was almost seven. Dressing with efficient precision in clothing suitable for exploration, he had just enough time left to walk the short hallway and tap on Cat and Evelyn's door at precisely seven.

Cat opened the door with a smile, looking wide awake and fresh; her long, red hair tied back from her face in her usual ponytail. "Good morning, Omar. Did you want to come in?"

He shook his head. "No, I'll wait out here."

She nodded, looking over her shoulder briefly before turning back to him and rolling her eyes. "Okay, well in that case, Evelyn will be another five minutes. She's not really a morning person."

"No problem." He found himself smiling unexpectedly at the note in her voice.

It struck him for the first time that these women were family, even though they looked so different. Part of the knot he'd been carrying inside since discovering Zahara missing eased. With friends like family, he knew the women would do everything possible to get Zahara back, and for the first time, he began to hope.

"We'll be right there," Cat said, shutting the door with a gentle click.

Omar walked over to the hall window and leaned on the wall beside it. Closing his eyes, he allowed himself to think of her face. Her eyes had the gentle darkness of rich soil in the spring and her smile shone as bright as the sun, lighting his heart. Her hair had rippled, even tied back and covered, with the soft beauty of the night.

He hadn't realized how cold he'd been until she brought summer back into his life. The cruelty of barely meeting her and having her torn away was hard for him to process. He wanted to spend more time with her and get to know her, to see if they could have a future together.

It was gnawing and unbearable to think he'd merely been granted a glimpse and fate had once again planned for him to be left alone.

"Sorry about the wait." Evelyn entered the hallway, appearing not the slightest bit sorry as Cat shut the door behind her.

He noticed their packed bags and raised his eyebrows. "You are ready to leave?"

Evelyn nodded. He noticed dark circles under her eyes and realized she wasn't as cool and collected as she appeared.

"Yup. We'll eat breakfast, but I'll wait to tell you what I learned last night until we get back in the Jeep. Too much potential for eavesdroppers."

They made short work of breakfast and were in the vehicle barely thirty minutes later. Omar drove as Evelyn sat in the front passenger's seat, elevated to shotgun in Zahara's absence because she was the one with the story. Cat leaned forward from the back to listen intently.

When Omar couldn't wait any longer, he prompted Evelyn. "Sorry to be so blunt, but I need to know what you found out."

"I understand. I guess I'll start at the beginning. I spoke with Robin last night. As we'd wondered, he had an inkling this was going to happen. It was why he directed us to Petra but also the reason he wanted us all together. He knew we'd be needed to get her back, although he didn't know how or when she'd disappear. He thought our plan to return where she was last seen is good, but he couldn't give me much more in the way of direction."

She stopped, rubbing her forehead. She looked tired today, evidence of her late night dream endeavors visible today. But the little insight she'd gained didn't make Omar feel any better, and he gripped the steering wheel tightly to channel his disappointment away from his voice.

"That's it?"

"He said he'd stay in touch." Evelyn frowned at Cat's squeak of disapproval. "He said he'll come when it's time. In the meanwhile, we're on our own."

Omar clenched his jaw. No; Zahara was the one on her own, not them. He didn't know how he'd manage it, but one way or another, he was going to get her back.

Even if he had to kill someone or die trying.

CHAPTER 13

With the acceptance Marwan was truly gone, Reema sprang into action.

"Quickly. We must arrange everything perfectly if we hope to stand a chance at succeeding. Zahara, read the ingredients out loud."

Zahara looked at the book, nonplussed. Thankfully, Marwan had left it open to the correct page and she leaned close, squinting as she sounded the words out and tried to make sense of them.

"Well, the amulet..."

It was a delaying tactic she'd learned from her brothers, but it helped her calm down as she tried to get a handle on the foreign handwriting. She tilted her head side to side a few times before making out another word.

"Zeafran"

Reema nodded, going to the kitchen and coming back with the yellow spice.

"How much?"

Zahara groaned. "Umm, ten threads, maybe?" Zahara squinted again then nodded. "Yes, ten looks right. Okay, it also wants three dates."

Reema went back to the kitchen. Each time Zahara called out a new ingredient, she grabbed the item and placed it neatly in a row on the table beside her. After ten minutes or so, Zahara reached the end of the page.

"Okay, that looks like all the ingredients. It says something about a large mixing bowl, and has a picture of what it's supposed to look like. Do you have anything like this?"

Reema looked at the diagram Zahara was tapping. It was hand drawn and to Zahara, closely resembled what years of movies told her a witch's cauldron should look like, but smaller. Next to that was another picture of a silver mixing spoon encrusted with four semi-precious stones.

"Marwan has a collection of items he uses for magic. Anything he has will be in the trunk where he kept the book." Reema went to the trunk and returned with the bowl and the spoon, along with several small sticks.

Zahara whistled. "Wow, that is some pricey looking paraphernalia."

Reema looked at her with confusion. "I am sorry, but I do not understand."

Zahara waved her hand. "Nothing. Don't worry about it. Just a figure of speech. Okay, so now we have all the ingredients; we need to use them in the right order. Each step has certain conditions which need to be followed."

Zahara reread the passage out loud on how the ingredients were supposed to be assembled, watching as Reema carefully added each item as she spoke. Once everything was in the cauldron, she instructed her on how to stir.

"You must blend the mixture with a silver spoon and make exactly eighty-eight clockwise circles then stop, followed by stirring another eighty-eight times counterclockwise."

Reema began to stir without questioning, counting under her breath until she reached the required number.

Zahara remembered what Marwan had said about Reema's mother helping. Currently, she was sitting quietly with Haytham on the couch. He'd slept through the earlier excitement in the way only a baby could. She wasn't sure what the older woman would be needed to help with unless it was keeping the child occupied, as the recipe was pretty easy so far.

Shrugging, she looked at Reema and saw she'd finished counting out the stirs and was waiting for further direction.

"What shall we do next?"

Zahara traced the words on the page, trying to decide if she was reading it right.

"I think this says to let it sit for exactly three hours. At that point, the amulet is supposed to be dipped in the mixture while we say a prayer to activate it."

Reema sighed. "So long? What do we do while it simmers?"

Zahara shrugged, trying not to feel nervous at the delay. "I guess we wait."

Reema sat on the cushion beside her mother and Zahara followed, but after a few minutes, her inner restlessness forced her to get up again.

"I want to see what's happening outside. Will you be okay?" It had been so quiet since they'd started the spell Zahara almost felt silly asking.

Reema looked startled, then glanced at her son before she replied. "I think so. Marwan warded this place to be invisible to anyone without invitation. We're safer in here than outside. I wish he had stayed," she lamented. "Men. They can't sit and wait out the threat, they must rise to defeat it or forever feel less than."

Zahara nodded, but wasn't sure she agreed with Reema's assertion the inability to wait was only a male trait. She understood exactly why he'd gone out to fight. It was what you did to protect those you loved, and likely partly why she was so restless herself.

Reema gave Zahara a wistful look. "He ran away once for me. Now that Abbas has found us, he will not run again. While I wish he had stayed here, I understand why he went to fight. We'll never be safe until Abbas is dead or defeated."

"In that case, I'm going to see if I can find Marwan. Maybe I can help him."

Now that she knew the tent was an island of safety, she couldn't sit and wait to see what happened. She had to see for herself what was going on outside.

Reema appeared horrified at the idea. "What if you are injured? Women shouldn't fight, especially when the matter is between two men."

Zahara scoffed. "Please. I have three brothers. I'm more than capable of fighting with men. My friends and I have had plenty of battles, so I'm confident in my abilities, thank you very much. But don't worry, I'm not going to go blazing in like an idiot. I'll go in fox form and stay hidden until I get a lay of the land. Marwan may need assistance."

Zahara didn't mention the other thought which crossed her mind. *And no one should die alone.* With her mind made up, she transformed.

"I'm leaving the necklace with you, in case I am delayed. When exactly three hours have passed, you must place the amulet in the mixture and wait."

"For what?" Reema asked.

Zahara shrugged. "I'm not entirely sure. The spell sounds like you'll know when it's done. Maybe it will absorb all the liquid, or send a flash out, or something. Just watch it closely. I'll be back as soon as I can. If Abbas looks like he's coming this way, I'll try to lead him away. Okay?"

Reema looked doubtful. "If you're sure. May Allah protect you."

Zahara bobbed her head. Her large ears twitching at the sounds outside, she darted away.

CHAPTER 14

Zahara crept out into the dusty air. Rubble had begun to settle on the ground but the air still hung heavily around her. The quaint pond and garden now looked dull, covered by silt and small rocks. It was like the aftermath of a bomb explosion, with all of the previous charm trapped under the debris.

Brushing aside her disappointment at the destruction of Reema's idyllic hiding spot, she padded down the path she remembered from the trip in. When she glanced back over her shoulder at the solitary tent, she could see it was similarly dull and dingy, but intact.

Hopefully whatever spell Marwan cast will hold. I'd really like to make it home in one piece, and my ticket back is inside that tent.

Careful to make as little noise as possible, Zahara moved further away from the tent. A sudden commotion erupted just past the rock face hiding the small sanctuary, and she slunk closer, pausing to sniff the air behind a small outcropping of rocks. Her nose twitched at the scent of strong magic in the air.

The smell of lightning and fire told her Abbas was close.

She slunk on her belly nearer to the edge and caught her breath at what she saw in front of her. She'd thought Marwan powerful when she'd first seen him in the tent, but it was nothing compared to how he looked now.

His green eyes glowed almost as brightly as the amulet while his robes swirled around him. She was struck by the memory of how Gandalf, the wizard in *Lord of the Rings,* had looked when he'd been in the underground tunnels. Marwan had the same fire in his expression and was just as impressive.

Unfortunately, the other jinn appeared far more terrifying. He had a hard, angry face with slashes of dark black eyebrows matching the hair which fell over his glowing yellow eyes and trailed uncovered down his back, writhing like a living thing in the wind that had been stirred up around the two jinn as they fought.

Without warning, he threw a ball of fire at Marwan.

Marwan fell, surprising a small yip out of Zahara. Her heart sank when he didn't immediately get up. She whipped her head back to Abbas in time to see him forming another ball and moved instinctively.

Racing in between the two jinn, Zahara zigzagged, catching Abbas by surprise. He threw the ball at her instead and she dodged it by inches. The heat grazed her tail with a searing pain and she yelped, but a quick glance revealed only a few singed hairs.

Racing forward, she continued to zig zag, hoping to keep Abbas' gaze off Marwan, who was now struggling to get up. If she could draw his attention away long enough, maybe he'd have a chance to recover and escape.

When she peered back this time, Abbas had lost interest, shifting his focus back to his efforts to destroy Marwan. At least he was standing again, but he didn't look good. He was swaying with exhaustion or injury, maybe both, she wasn't sure. It appeared he was trying to cast a spell of his own but he seemed too weak, and she didn't think he was going to complete it in time.

Abbas formed another ball, this one a black ball of dark energy, which caused a strange stillness to fall over her. It didn't look like fire, or anything else she'd ever seen.

It looked like what she imagined death would look like.

She screamed out a warning just as the ball of energy hit Marwan. He looked at Zahara as it impacted him and his face filled with an unearthly calm eve as his eyes met hers with a world of despair trapped inside.

"Tell them I love them. Keep them safe."

A tear tracked down her furry jowls as the dark ball spread out and absorbed him, covering every inch until nothing remained. Just like that, Marwan vanished.

Rage and sorrow mixed and the rumble of a growl began in her chest, increasing in intensity until Abbas noticed her again. With his focus no longer required to deal with Marwan, he turned his attention to Zahara.

Staring down his nose, he examined her with a look of disgust and vague curiosity. "And what clever pet are you, little one?" He spoke as though he half-expected her to answer but without pausing long enough for her to reply, even had she felt like it. "Are you this dead fool's familiar? Or are you something...more? *Hmmmm*?"

Zahara wasn't about to give him the satisfaction of an answer. If he thought her a pet, she knew he would act differently than if he thought she was part of the family he'd sworn to destroy. So, she took her cue from him and acted as any good pet would, baring her teeth and letting another growl escape.

He strode toward her without any trace of concern, a cruel laugh bubbling up as he neared. "Oh, you're going to avenge his death? How sweet. How about I allow you to join him forever instead?"

Zahara's eyes widened as the same dark energy, the energy she'd watched destroy Marwan, filled his hand. Without wasting time, she charged at him with her teeth bared.

She lunged and snapped, latching onto his ankle and managing to savage it for a brief instant before taking off in the opposite direction from the tent. She knew she couldn't beat him, but if she could lead him away from the others, maybe he wouldn't look for them.

If she was lucky, he might think Marwan had been there alone. *Maybe.*

Her breath was becoming labored and her throat felt raspy from running while fear choked her. She glanced back. He was gaining. Concentrating on her surroundings, she sensed a weak spot in the ground underneath the area Abbas was gliding rapidly toward her along.

As he stepped forward, she caused the earth to collapse underneath his foot and close around his bloody ankle, trapping him. She knew it was only a temporary hold and kept running, her only goal now to get as far away from Reema as she could.

Suddenly, the sound of dogs baying filled her ears.

Fear supercharged her feet.

Dogs were her weakness. They were as fast as she was but stronger. She wasn't sure if he'd read her mind or if he sent them after her due to the way dogs loved to chase down prey, but it didn't matter. She needed to avoid them at all costs. Putting her head down she ran faster.

The sound of the dogs became louder as they grew closer. She was losing ground and bitterness rose in her throat.

Searching wildly for a place to hide, she raced across the sand and rocky ground with speed only a small animal terrified for its life can muster.

Her heart beat madly as the dogs drew nearer.

She could smell them next to her now. She couldn't escape and the hopelessness almost choked her. Just as she felt the hot breath of her pursuers brush her heels, she saw a lone tree ahead, hanging precariously over a rocky outcropping.

She raced toward it, knowing her life depended on it. Luck was with her when she spied a small hole in the base.

Thank all the gods.

She darted inside just as teeth grazed her left back leg, scraping but not catching hold. The hole didn't stop though, and she tumbled down into the darkness.

The dogs howled in anger, snuffling and pawing at the base of the tree as they barked wildly in the night, pointing out the location of their elusive target to their master.

But Zahara couldn't hear them any longer.

CHAPTER 15

Omar looked around the cave. He hadn't been to this place in years. He'd never seen the attraction of Petra, finding the deadness of the place too unsettling for him to appreciate the beauty of the carvings on the walls. As an earth mage and a child of nature, with his other form that of a fox who needed to run, he needed a connection with the land.

To him, Petra was a graveyard and the land around it was a corpse.

As it had always left him cold, he'd preferred to spend his time in Amman when he needed to get supplies or a change of scenery, even though Petra was closer. At least that city hummed with life, even if the magic of the earth was covered up like an old woman in winter.

The cave he was in now struck him the way Petra always did. It was dull and lifeless. Any magic that had once existed here was absent now, with nothing to look at or sense but sand and rocks. Even so, according to her friends, somehow there had been enough magic here for Zahara to disappear.

"Tell me again what happened," he asked. "And be precise."

He turned to look at her friends. They were nice women, but he felt nothing in their presence. Not like what he'd felt standing beside Zahara. He needed to find her. To get her back so he would know if what he'd felt had been real or just his imagination after being alone for so long.

"We were standing right here." Cat pointed to a spot beside him. "Zahara was where you are right now, I was across from her, and Evelyn was here."

Cat waved Evelyn over to assume the positions they'd been standing in at the time of the disappearance, placing Omar where Zahara had been.

"Zahara had just put on her amulet at the time," Evelyn recalled. "It started to glow a really bright green. I remember she looked surprised, then poof! She vanished. I'm not sure how she had time to scream. Maybe I heard my own shock because it all happened in an instant, like she popped out of existence instead of fading away."

Omar nodded. He wasn't sure how it was possible, but clearly her disappearance was tied to the amulet. "Where is the necklace now?" He knew even before he asked what the answer would be, but wanted them to confirm his suspicions.

Cat shrugged. "Probably with her. It was gone as soon as she was. Once Zahara vanished, the green light went out, and it was just Evelyn and I standing here looking confused."

"Okay, well, that narrows it down. I think we can all agree she's gone because of the amulet. Now we need to find out where she went and how to get her back."

He walked around the cave, rubbing his chin as he paced. He didn't have much experience with magic outside that of his own earth type, but he remembered a man from childhood who'd bragged about being able to transport himself from place to place with an amulet. He'd always thought it the boasting of a man who lacked true magic, but now he wondered if it was possible, and if Zahara had somehow done the same thing.

He wished he had a better idea how that type of magic worked. Did he need the same amulet for her to return? Or was it possible to cast another spell, or use a different amulet to bring her back? He sighed, dropping down on a rock in a corner and cradling his head in his hands. It seemed hopeless.

A familiar voice broke into his despair. "Nothing is ever truly hopeless, my friend."

"Robin? Old friend, is it really you?"

Omar jerked his head up, springing up and opening his arms wide when he saw Robin smiling back at him. They gave each other a hug, and Robin clapped him vigorously on the back before pulling away to wink at Cat and Evelyn.

"Robin! It's so great to see you!" Cat smiled.

Evelyn's smile was a little smug. "Thanks for coming, love. It looks like we're in need of assistance. But how did..." She trailed off, then shook her head. Holding up a hand, with a smile she stopped him. "Never mind, the details don't matter. I'm just happy you were able to get away."

Robin gave Cat a bow before sweeping Evelyn into a warm embrace, spinning her around once before putting her down but keeping an arm around her shoulder instead of letting go entirely.

"I called in a favor, or was it two?" Robin's eyes twinkled as he spoke.

Relief washed over Omar. If Robin was here, it would all work out. It had the last time. If Robin was here, he had faith he'd see Zahara again soon.

Omar bowed before looking up eagerly. "Thank you for coming, old friend. Your presence is much appreciated. We are in your hands. What should we do first?"

"The first thing we should do is sit down. I'm starving and would like to eat. Do you happen to have any cheese or honey? It's been ages since anyone brought me offerings."

Cat raised an eyebrow. "Is that statement directed at me? I bring something nearly every time I'm near a gate, unless I didn't know one was going to pop out at me."

Robin laughed at Cat, flicking the tip of her nose. "Of course not, Lady Firebird. You are extremely good at remembering to honor me. But food first before we discuss strategy is always my first step."

He plopped down into a cross-legged position on the floor of the cave. He looked like a little bird, waiting to be fed. Cat and Evelyn giggled and sat down while Omar looked through his supplies to find the requested items.

"Here you are. I hope these meet with your approval."

Robin smiled, answering by digging into the cheese and honey sandwiches. Omar waited patiently, but his worry for Zahara felt like acid in his stomach and he had little interest in the food. Finally, Robin sat back and sighed, patting his stomach with pleasure.

"That was most appreciated, my friend. Now, onward! Time to discuss the riddle of the little fox's disappearance." Robin looked at the eager faces sitting around him and rubbed his hands together before placing them on his knees. "Let's start at the beginning, shall we?"

From past experience, Omar knew Robin was a great storyteller, but it was best to get comfortable because he could be a little long-winded. Cat and Evelyn groaned as they settled themselves down for a long story, but Omar didn't mind. He'd grown up listening to Robin's tall tales and had always loved them. He rested his chin on his hand, waiting for Robin to continue.

"In the beginning, Petra was an oasis in the heart of the desert. The Nabatean people who lived here were wise and worked together to create a beautiful green space in the midst of a dry land. They knew where to find the water sleeping and how best to use it to shape their city into a paradise while conserving the scarce resources. For years they created miracles, protecting both the water in the desert and the magic in the earth."

Robin paused to look at Cat. "As Cat may have already mentioned, Western history records a devastating earthquake in 363 AD." Robin shook his head. "But in reality, it was no earthquake."

Cat leaned in closer. "It wasn't? I knew it! Is that why the land feels dead? We can't sense any magic here."

Robin nodded. "Exactly. The devastation was entirely due to the actions of one jinn, known only by the name Abbas. He was very powerful, but greedy and immoral. He wished to have all the magic for himself. During the years he was active, he cut a wide swath through all of those who held magic at that time, killing them or worse. The Nabateans did their best to stop him, but they failed. They had already lost control of their land to the Romans years earlier, and when Abbas violently tore the magic from the land that day, their civilization collapsed entirely."

Evelyn interrupted. "Is this what happened to Zahara? Did she fall into a hole? Did Abbas take her?"

Robin shook his head. "Not exactly. Abbas had achieved all he desired except for one thing. After Petra, only small pockets of magic remained and by then, he was nearly immortal. Even with his power though, he still wasn't happy. He looked across the world and saw the Ottoman Empire stretching over the land and became obsessed with the affairs of humans."

Cat nodded. "He worked his way in the court of Suleyman, didn't he?"

"Yes. But one jinn stood in his way. He was a powerful jinn in his own right, but it was the power of his soul, not his magic, that blocked Abbas' machinations."

Omar was enthralled. "How could one jinn manage that?"

"This jinn, Marwan, blocked Abbas by his simple refusal to marry his daughter and unite his power with Abbas' family line."

Omar's mouth dropped as comprehension settled in. "Because of Marwan's magic, Abbas wasn't the only jinn who could control humans. This caused huge problems, I'm sure."

Robin nodded. "Yes, it did. Not only did Marwan refuse to marry his daughter, Abbas knew of a prophecy, one which Marwan was unaware of. You see, it had been foretold that only a descendant of Marwan's would be the one to control the land. Abbas planned to rule through the child, but in order for that to happen, he needed the child to be his own grandchild."

Evelyn raised an eyebrow. "I'm guessing that didn't happen?"

"You are correct," Robin sighed. "Love was more powerful than even the lust Abbas had for power. Marwan fell in love with a local Bedouin girl and called off his nuptials to the daughter of the jinn. He ran away in the night, crushing Abbas's plans to rule. From then on, Abbas swore his eternal revenge against Marwan and all of his descendants."

"Zahara is Marwan's descendant, isn't she?" Omar's face drooped as what they were up against settled into the pit in his stomach. With that kind of backstory, she was in grave danger for sure.

A sad smile crossed Robin's face. "She is. That is why she has been drawn into the eternal fight between the two jinn. In order for her to return safely to our time, she must defeat Abbas on her own. The most we can do is to ensure the portal is safe for her to travel."

"Our time?" Omar sputtered. "She's stuck in the past?"

"Yes."

Cat looked stunned. "Are you saying we...just sit here and wait?"

Robin shrugged. "Basically. It won't be that easy, of course. As the battle rages on her end, we will be tested on ours. Ripples of this amount of power create small eddies and breaches in how reality works. At times, my duty to the earth supersedes my duty to my own small island. This is one of them. I am here to aid you in this matter because of the importance of getting her back and protecting the other humans in the area. We must be ready to deal with the minions Abbas will send to try to keep Zahara from returning, and it will challenge us all to our limits."

Omar threw his shoulders back. "We will be ready. What should we watch for?"

"Be on guard against smoke, wind, or anything else outside of what is expected for the natural world. You must keep the cave safe. Zahara will need a place to return and the amulet will try to bring her back to the exact place she left."

Evelyn looked at Robin curiously. "Okay, that's clear enough. I know we can handle standing our ground, but what are you going to do?"

Robin winked, and Omar recognized the familiar smile which always spelled trouble.

"I've already made this a protected area so humans will not interfere. Now I'm going to say hello to an old friend."

CHAPTER 16

*Z*ahara blinked her eyes in the darkness. Her head was pounding. A whimper escaped as she tried to focus on the ground she was lying on. Had she blacked out in the fall? She didn't recognize her surroundings. But even as she began to panic, the memory of the chase flooded back in pieces. Dogs had been chasing her. Abbas was after her. He'd killed Marwan.

She groaned and lay back, panting slightly from the movement and gave in to her emotions. After a few minutes of self-pity and tears, she berated herself. Crying would get her nothing but a headache. She needed to do something, but what? With her mind fuzzy from the fall, it was hard to remember what her plan had been. She knew she was supposed to do something.

The amulet!

She sat up, hearing her paws scrabbling on the hard ground in the silence. The sound of the dogs had vanished, but that didn't mean they weren't waiting for her outside of where it was she'd fallen. She needed to be careful, but she also needed to get back to Reema and complete the spell. It was even more important now Marwan was dead because only Reema and her mother were left to protect Haytham. If anything happened to him, Zahara and her family wouldn't exist anymore.

Her nose twitched as a new odor rose.

It smelled like...foxes.

This time as she looked around, she glimpsed a faint light. It was in the opposite direction from where she'd fallen into the hole and she limped toward it cautiously, smelling her way as she listened for the sound of anyone approaching.

She emerged into a small cave to see a family of foxes huddled together. The minute she appeared, they shrank away. She ducked her head down and waited, trying to look as non-threatening as possible. After a minute, one of the larger foxes stepped toward her.

As its nose twitched, assessing her, she sent it a thought, hoping it would understand.

Please, do not be afraid. I mean you no harm. I need help.

The fox, who she saw in the dim light was a red fox, not fennec like herself, tilted its head from side to side as it examined her. At first, she feared it didn't understand her plea, and relief filled her when it answered.

What is it you want, outsider? You are not a true fox. The stink of magic is upon you.

Zahara ducked her head lower.

You are correct. I have earth magic, but I am not of the earth. I am the descendant of a human and a jinn. The jinn who was my ancestor has been struck down by an evil jinn who means to destroy my entire family. I need to get back to the home of my ancestor to protect the child who will become my great, great, great, grandfather. Can you help me?

The fox narrowed his eyes and padded back to the others. Zahara waited breathlessly as the skulk of foxes considered her question. She knew animals disliked magic, with its tendency to go badly for them, but after much deliberation, the red fox returned.

We have discussed it and have agreed. I will lead you through the hidden passages to the tent where the humans are. What you do from there is your own problem. We do not want any part in your fight but are all too aware of this jinn. He has caused great destruction to our land and is no friend of ours. Lead him away, and we will consider the scales even.

Zahara nodded, bowing at the shoulders to place her head almost on the ground.

Thank you. Your assistance is much appreciated.

Come then. The fox gestured with his head. *We must leave now, before the dogs return. I want no harm to befall my kin while I lead you back to yours.*

Zahara followed the fox without question. She was aware what a huge leap of faith the fox was taking, leaving its family to help her. If it hadn't been for the stench of dark magic drifting down from the hole, she was sure she'd have been out of luck.

As they walked deeper into the darkness, Zahara was grateful for her night vision. As a human she would have been blind, but as a fox, the faint glow of daylight ahead was enough for her to pick her way through the narrow passage.

They walked for what felt like at least an hour before the fox stopped sharply, almost causing Zahara to bump into him. She caught herself in the nick of time and watched as his whiskers twitched. She took a quick sniff of her own and felt her spirits rise. Humans!

The red fox crept forward more slowly now, and Zahara followed suit. The light grew brighter until they came around the next curve to a small opening. In front of them the moon and stars shone bright in the sky. Her stomach dropped.

What time was it? Am I already too late?

The red fox turned to her.

This is where I leave you. Be safe.

Zahara nodded her thanks.

And you as well. I will never forget your kindness.

With a bob of acknowledgment, the fox disappeared back into the darkness of the tunnel.

Zahara sat at the mouth of the hole and took stock of her surroundings. The faint sound of water in the pond was audible to her left and she knew she was only a few feet away from the tent. She sniffed, but there was no hint of any of the terrible magic she'd smelled earlier. There was no trace of the dogs either, so she crept along the cave wall and circled the clearing until she finally arrived at the tent.

Hoping against hope she wasn't too late, Zahara nosed the door open.

CHAPTER 17

"Praise Allah, you have returned!" Reema met Zahara at the doorway.

Zahara shifted back to human barely in time to brace herself against Reema's entire weight. She cringed inwardly at how filthy she was. There was no way the dirt she'd accumulated in her trek wouldn't transfer to Reema as well, but the other woman didn't seem to care.

The way she clung to her told Zahara that more clearly than words could have.

"Did I miss it? Am I too late?" Zahara had no idea how long she'd been unconscious, only that it was night and while she'd been gone, Marwan had died.

Reema shook her head. "No, not yet. We still have a few minutes left." She paused, looking at Zahara with fear and anticipation. Something in Zahara's face must have told her what had happened, because her voice became thin and reedy. "Marwan?"

Zahara couldn't speak. The lump in her throat was too thick. She shook her head instead and watched as Reema's face crumpled.

Tears leaked out of her eyes as she worked to compose herself. Zahara wouldn't have thought less of her if she cried or fell to the ground. She wanted to do those things herself. But Reema didn't even lose herself the way she had when Marwan had first left. She just nodded and took a deep breath, wiping her tears away as she lifted her chin.

Her eyes hardened. "Abbas?"

Zahara shook her head. "Still out there, somewhere. I managed to distract him, but it wasn't enough. Marwan fought bravely."

Zahara thought of the ball of black Abbas had thrown. What was that thing? And how had it killed Marwan? She returned her attention to Reema, trying to push the terrible sight out of her mind.

"I was only able to get away because a family of foxes who helped me. Abbas set dogs on me." Zahara wrinkled her nose, unable to keep a shiver from traveling down her spine at the memory.

Reema pursed her lips. "Even more crucial for us to finish the spell. Marwan said it could trap Abbas for a million years, which is only what he deserves. Death is too good for him and not nearly long enough. We must be ready to fight Abbas. Without my husband to protect us, I shall be the protector of this family." She stared into the bubbling pot as if transfixed. "Nothing appears to have changed since we first put the ingredients into it. *Umi* was kind enough to watch the liquid while I rested and fed Haytham. "

Zahara nodded. "I will be ready. But first, I need to eat. I'm starving. The fight and transformations have sapped much of my energy. I'll need food if I'm going to have any chance of surviving when I meet him again."

Reema nodded and went to the kitchen, deftly placing food on a plate and setting it at the small table when she was done. Zahara dug in ravenously, not stopping until the plate was empty. Pushing it in front of her, she smiled.

"Thank you. I wish I could have done more for Marwan. I've never seen anything like what Abbas threw at him in the fight." She shuddered at the memory. The dark magic she'd witnessed would haunt her dreams. "It was like he held the absence of life in his hands, so dark, powerful, and final."

Reema's face was stoic. "That likely is exactly what you saw. He sucked this place dry of its magic, hundreds of years ago. That kind of evil is hard to come back from. It taints everything the user does for the remainder of their days on earth. Most individuals would never chance it, but for those who worship power over their place in the universe, sadly, this cost is not a consideration or hinderance."

Zahara sighed. Life would be so much easier if all people and creatures, magical and otherwise, worked towards unity and harmony. But while she wished evil didn't exist, she knew there would always be those who were solely out for themselves, and others who reveled in working for the darkness.

A familiar smell wafted through one of the open tent flaps, causing Zahara to whirl around. "Reema, he's here!"

The other woman paled. "How? Marwan hid us. He said our home is heavily warded against all detection."

Zahara shook her head. "I don't know. Either Abbas can see past the protections, or they failed when Marwan died. I'll lead him away—you have to be ready to put the amulet in when it's time."

Reema shook her head. "No! You need to be here for that part. It won't work without you."

"We don't know that for certain. What we do know is if Abbas gets in, you and Haytham are dead, and the spell will certainly not be completed. We have to take the chance."

Zahara transformed quickly, grateful she was replete from her meal and as ready as possible to attempt to outwit Abbas. She twitched her nose, wishing she could reassure Reema everything would be okay. "You can do this. Let me do what I can to make sure you are able to complete the spell."

Without waiting for a reply, she crept out the door of the tent and back into the night.

CHAPTER 18

"Man, I hate it when he does that," Cat grumbled, staring at the empty spot Robin had been standing in seconds before.

Evelyn laughed. "Oh, you know him." She shrugged before winking and giving Cat a naughty smile. "He likes to keep the mystery alive."

Omar watched the interplay between the two friends without speaking. He didn't want to interrupt what was obviously an ongoing debate about Robin. When Cat looked at him, her eyebrows lowered and her face clouded, she caught his patient expression and blushed.

"Sorry. I find it irritating he can't manage to say goodbye like a normal person." As soon as she spoke, she held up a hand. "I know, I know, he's not a normal person. Anyway, that's my problem, apparently."

Omar chuckled. "I know. It can be annoying but I'm used to it by now. It's not something that ever bothered me much. I figured out when I was still a kit that he leaves when he's finished talking. It's kept things easy for me. But regardless of small details such as manners, he brought up an important point. We need to be ready for anything. If Robin is able to come here now, it means that for whatever reason, magic is back. That's good for us, but also good for anyone or anything trying to impede Zahara's return. We can't let that happen."

"Of course," Evelyn replied. "What do you propose?"

He looked at the wide open mouth of the cave then surveyed the inside again before answering. "There's not much we can do about changing the cave. There's only the entrance we came in, so only one point to guard. That's good and bad. It's easier to make sure no one enters without us knowing, but that also means we could end up being trapped. The desert is unforgiving at the best of times, but if Robin expects an attack, things are likely going to get much worse. He doesn't believe in warning others about things that will happen far down the road."

"True," said Cat. "The last time he told us we were in danger it was like ten minutes before we were in the thick of it. So, does this mean magic is a go?"

Omar shrugged. "I'm sure your magic worked here before. For powers tied to earth magic like what Robin, Zahara, and myself possess, Petra's dead zone severely limits our abilities. We can still do things, it's just much harder. I think this means the area may have more of its own magic, in a way it hasn't since Abbas drained the place centuries ago."

Evelyn looked around the cave, her eyes fuzzy and swirling an opalescent color that surprised Omar. Earlier, they'd been a warm brown almost as beautiful as Zahara's. As he watched, she scanned the entire area, and when she answered, they had returned to their normal color. Had he imagined it?

"Yup, magic is back."

Cat cocked her head. "What do you mean?"

Evelyn pointed to an empty corner.

Omar squinted, but couldn't see anything. "I don't know what you are pointing at."

"There's a dead soldier over there. Roman, I'd guess by the clothing, but I'm not the history major."

Cat sighed. "Well, this was a Roman tomb at one point, so you're likely right about his origin. I'm going to stand in the doorway and guard the cave from there, okay? Unless you want to take point, Evelyn? If you're seeing ghosts again, maybe it's better if you stay further out of the cave?"

Cat looked at Evelyn, and he saw the worry as Evelyn continued looking at the empty space before finally shaking her head.

"Nah, I'm fine. Ghosts don't bother me much anymore. I've gotten used to them over the last few years. The trick is to remember to ignore them. They just have issues with reality."

Evelyn rolled her eyes and Omar caught a glimpse of darkness behind the nonchalance that made him think she wasn't as unaffected as she was trying to appear.

"You go ahead. I'll see if Mr. Roman Ghosty here can fill me in on anything relevant, or if he can only talk about himself like all the others."

Omar watched Cat and Evelyn head to opposite sides of the cave, which left him alone in the middle. Closing his eyes, he took a deep breath and inhaled the scent of dirt and desert air. As he focused, the familiar dry, lifeless air suddenly came alive with the faintest tingle of magic.

He opened his eyes and crouched down, looking at the earth more closely. He could appreciate a subtle green shimmer beginning to spread over the dirt-packed floor. He concentrated harder and added his own energy, trying to grow it. A moment later, small green shoots sprang out of the ground and began to stretch themselves up, questing for sunshine.

"Cool!" Evelyn had noticed what he was doing and clapped her hands at the sight of the small sprout.

He flashed her a triumphant smile as he sat cross-legged on the ground. "Thanks. Anything from your end?"

Evelyn shook her head, looking disappointed. "Nope. Conceited, like most ghosts. All I could get from him is a 'woe is me, I'm so dead, darkness, blah, blah.' You keep doing that though— I want to see what else you can do."

He nodded and rested the backs of his hands on his knees, closing his eyes again. This time, he focused not on the green plants themselves, but on the aura of life he sensed within them. He wanted to have as much positive magic surrounding them as possible for when Zahara returned.

And maybe a pretty flower to give her, too.

"Guys! Something's coming! Look!"

Omar's concentration broke as Cat shouted. The plant he was working on collapsed. He hated being interrupted, but the concern in her voice told him it was important. As he neared Cat's position at the entrance, he saw a large black cloud racing toward them.

"What is *that*?" Evelyn came to stand next to Omar and Cat.

"It feels like darkness," Cat whispered, watching the cloud billowing like smoke as it approached across the ground outside. "Like a larger, scarier version of the soulless guys we fought before."

"I think you're right," Evelyn said. "I wonder if a nice wall of fire would be a good option right about now. At least ten feet away though. I don't want you cutting off our oxygen supply."

Cat narrowed her eyes against the wind that had begun to pick up as the dark wall of cloud neared the cave. "Okay, but stand back, just in case. It's been a while since I've done anything big with fire."

They stepped back inside the cave as Cat moved to the center of the opening and walked out to a point about ten feet away. Just as the dark cloud looked like it would swoop down and swallow her, Cat exploded into a fiery being.

Startled, Omar stepped back. His mouth dropped when he recognized the shape of a phoenix appear where Cat's body had been. She glowed as an inferno surrounded her and when he looked at the wall she'd raised, he realized it was working. With awe, he watched the previously quiet, history-obsessed woman he'd travelled with over the last few days become an angel of fire.

He stood beside Evelyn and watched while Cat successfully held off the darkness. Her features were mostly obscured by the fire, but he could see the dark cloud fading like ink diluted in the sea as she worked.

"She's doing it!" He tapped his fist on Evelyn's shoulder in his excitement before grimacing an apology.

Evelyn nodded, shooting him a grin. "For now. But we need to be ready to catch her. I've seen her do this before and it's going to completely blow through her energy. She'll collapse the second her fire goes out. Get food ready—I'll watch and call when I need you."

He nodded and grabbed his bag, feeling useful as he set up a quick meal on the picnic blanket on the cave floor. As Evelyn predicted, the dark cloud was swallowed by the fire, and the second it vanished, Cat collapsed into Evelyn's waiting arms.

"How're you feeling, tall buddy?" Evelyn asked, as she helped Cat inside.

"Burnt out, heh heh heh," Cat joked, her voice weak.

She earned an eye roll so large from Evelyn he was surprised she didn't hurt herself, but she helped Cat sit on the blanket before letting go. He then watched the tired redhead literally devour everything he'd placed in front of her. He was sure his surprise was evident, never having seen a woman eat so much food before.

"Um, do you need more?"

"No, thanks. I just need to lay down for a minute and catch my breath. You guys hold the fort?"

Cat flopped onto her backpack as she spoke, using it as a pillow. Even before they answered, her eyes closed and she was out cold.

Omar stood up and walked to the front of the cave. "I guess the next wave is on us?"

Evelyn shrugged. "Guess so. I hope Robin hurries up with his 'old friend' though, cause I think we'll need him sooner rather than later if that was just the first shot from the opposition." She glanced worriedly at the horizon. "That was the largest amount of darkness I've seen in a long while. The amount of power Cat burned through blocking it was enormous. Her aura drained almost completely." She bit her lip, her eyes shadowed with worry. "The last time that happened, she dusted like a real phoenix and had to rise from her ashes. We don't have time right now for her to need that level of recovery."

Omar took a deep breath. "We *will* keep this cave safe. Zahara must return. Whatever it takes, I will do it. I have faith Robin will return on time."

Evelyn tilted her head, pressing her lips together as their eyes met. "I sure hope you're right. I mean, I love the guy, but he hasn't always been there for me in the past. I just hope this doesn't end up being one of those times."

Omar looked at Evelyn with surprise, but the closed look on her face made him decide he didn't want to ask what she meant.

It sounded like a long story for another time.

CHAPTER 19

Zahara's paws made no sound as she crept across the sand. The bright moon gave her more than enough light to see by, even though what she saw almost made her wish it hadn't been present.

Standing in the narrow passageway, Abbas was starkly highlighted against the backdrop of the rocks behind him. The glowing red eyes of the dogs who had chased her into the ground flanked him on both sides.

Clenching her teeth, she looked around and weighed her options.

Abbas and the dogs had blocked the hollow, so it was out as a means for escape. The tent behind her wasn't an option either, as the entire reason she was here was to buy time for Reema to complete the spell and keep Abbas away from Haytham.

To her right was the pond with the small vegetable patch, to her left was a solid wall of rock. She briefly considered her chances of successfully scaling the wall while Abbas watched, and immediately ruled it out. That definitely wouldn't work.

Her only option here, other than a direct assault against the jinn who'd killed an ancestor far more powerful than her, seemed limited to the vegetable patch. She measured the distance from the tent to the patch with her eyes. It would have to do.

Dashing toward the patch, adrenaline gave wings to her feet.

The dogs, scenting her, howled loudly and immediately scrambled after her. The distant sound of the same dark laughter she'd heard when Marwan died came to her on the breeze and her anger crested.

I'll show him.

She dashed between the plants in the garden and the scrubby brush that surrounded the area, carefully staying away from the pond. She might use it later, but right now she had another plan to trap the dogs.

Looking over her shoulder, she waited until they were almost on her heels before she halted and did an abrupt about-face. The dogs scattered in surprise when the small fox leapt at them, but not for long.

They were terrifying up close as they regrouped, with red demonic eyes and black triangles of ears pricked up and almost invisible against the night. One bit her on the haunch before she could duck and she yelped, hurrying to call on her magic before they could surround her.

The soft ground beside the pond collapsed, and the howls of the dogs tumbling into a crevice of her making echoed horrendously in the still of the night. Zahara closed her eyes and concentrated, trying not to let it bother her. Between the space of two heartbeats, she closed the ground over them. The sound halted.

Normally, she'd never use her magic against an animal, but these dogs had not been mere animals. Whatever Abbas had done to them or wherever he'd acquired them from, they had been as close to a demon as anything she'd ever encountered.

With the hell dogs taken care of, she limped under a bush to scout for Abbas. Unfortunately, he was closer than she expected.

His voice slid through the night, dark and velvety like coffee, sending prickles of cold down her back. "So, the pet fox has some earth magic, hmmmm? No wonder you are not dead yet. Clearly the unstable ground earlier was no coincidence."

He strode toward her on the path, his long, languorous steps betraying a complete lack of concern at the confirmation she wasn't a natural fox.

Zahara searched the ground beside her for anything to use as a weapon as she began to hyperventilate.

I'm so screwed. What could I possibly use to defeat him if Marwan couldn't?

Marwan knew spells, all Zahara had was...

Zahara bared her teeth. She may be little, but by damn, she was stubborn. She came toward Abbas, placing one cautious paw in front of another and tried not to limp too obviously.

He chuckled at the sight. "Oh, look at the little baby fox. How *precious*."

He hissed the word at her like an epithet, which had the likely unintended consequence of solidifying her will. It reminded her of something one of her brothers would have said if they'd been trying to intimidate or insult her.

And as always, it had the opposite effect of what was intended.

She stopped moving, planting her feet shoulder-width apart as she bared her teeth and growled. "I'm not going anywhere, Abbas."

Abbas yawned before making a show of brushing imaginary lint off his sleeve. His eyes sparkled in the dark. "So tiring, listening to the whining of dogs. Fox, dog, whatever. You are just a little...bitch."

Zahara narrowed her eyes. "Did you just call me a bitch?"

Abbas didn't answer. Using her anger against her as a distraction, she didn't realize he'd made one of the black fireballs from the battle with Marwan until he threw it. Off balance from her injury and inattention, she didn't manage to avoid it completely.

A gasp of pain escaped as the dark energy brushed her uninjured back leg and she reacted without thinking. Throwing herself under one of the bushes, she rolled and dashed as fast as she could through the tangled maze, impeding his view of her well enough to duck the second ball.

She continued to move without looking back and as she wove through the shrubs, they lit up behind her as he threw one ball after another. She ran as fast as she could toward the pond, darting in a zig-zag pattern to avoid the dark energy.

But he kept coming.

She felt like she was trapped in a horror movie where the dumb heroine was tripping and falling as the psychopath came for her. But Zahara was not a victim or a heroine. When she reached the edge of the pond, she whipped around to face him again.

Abbas cracked his neck then his fingers, lacing them together in front of his chest. "I'm truly going to enjoy this." He gave her a cruel smile filled with sharp, inhuman teeth and slowly licked his lips. "I wonder what roast fox tastes like?"

His evil chuckle filled the night as he made another fireball. But this time, instead of releasing it and hurling it at her, it winked out before he could wield it. His eyes widened with surprise as he looked down at his feet.

"What? No!"

Vines surrounded his body, snaking around his arms and legs. He struggled to break free but they tightened as Zahara continued to wrap them around every inch of his body, including his mouth when she saw him trying to speak.

Whether it was a spell or more smack, she didn't care. She didn't want him talking, period.

Once the vines were as tight as any zip-tie, she dropped the earth below him for good measure, burying him in the sand the way she had his demon dogs. Silence permeated the night.

The ground where he'd been was still for now, but Zahara wasn't fooled. He was far too powerful for her magic to hold him long. But maybe, just maybe, it would be enough time to save Reema and Haytham. She didn't bother to check her trap, knowing even a small delay could be the difference required for him to break out and capture them before they finished the spell.

She raced back to the tent where the others were hiding and her heart tripped at the sight of the dark, quiet home. She burst in, letting out a sigh of relief when she saw Reema and her mum standing beside the cauldron with the amulet in their joined hands.

Reema's startled gaze met Zahara. "You made it! Did you...is he?"

Zahara shook her head. "No, he's still out there. I bought us a few minutes, but he's on his way. Is it time?"

Reema nodded. "Yes. We were waiting for you to read the prayer. Remember, Marwan said it will be stronger if we say it together.

Zahara transformed back to her human shape and joined hands with Reema and her mum. They said a prayer which felt deceptively simple on paper, but as they chanted in unison, power crackled in the air.

Allah bless us,
Allah protect us
Place your power
into this vessel
no harm shall fall
no death shall pass
until one million years
or until the first
is the very last

The three women repeated the prayer eight times, then as one, they dropped the amulet into the now roiling waters of the cauldron.

At first, nothing happened. As they watched, the amulet began to glow and soak up the liquid. Within moments, the fluid had vanished, leaving the emerald winking up at them from the bottom of the cauldron, looking exactly the same as it had before they'd put it into the mixture.

Reema's hand shook as she lifted it out of the cauldron. Staring at the glowing emerald, she held it out to Zahara.

"Take it, Zahara. It is for you to wield."

Zahara knew the amulet was active now, in a way it hadn't been even when it had transported her here. It felt different, heavier somehow, and when it crossed her palm, she felt the tingle of power. "Thank you."

Her words had barely died away when a roar split the night.

The three women met each other's terrified eyes and Zahara instinctively placed the amulet around her neck.

Reema looked at the door and spoke the words they'd all been dreading. "He's here."

Transforming into a fox again, Zahara ducked under the table as Abbas burst into the tent.

CHAPTER 20

Omar looked at the sand swirling around the exterior of the cave and shook his head. "That isn't a normal sandstorm. It's another attack."

Cat was still sleeping off her earlier contribution to the protection of the cave but Evelyn stood when he spoke and came to look.

"Do you want me to take care of this?"

Omar shook his head. "No, I think given the earth nature of the storm I should be the one to deal with it. After all, earth is my realm. Can you make sure Cat is protected? I feel we'll need her powers again shortly."

"Gotcha. Holler if you need anything."

Evelyn returned to Cat and Omar closed his eyes, concentrating on the sand flying toward him.

Slowing his breathing, he waited until he could sense each grain of sand in the wave thrashing and spinning ever closer. Once he could feel them, he concentrated on laying each one down, picturing them lining up in a smooth sheet on the ground like he was ironing a blanket. When the roaring of the sand in his head calmed, he opened his eyes. He smiled with satisfaction as the wall of sand shimmered and smoothed out, mirroring what he'd created in his head and creating a uniform surface on the ground outside.

Once again, the desert returned to normal around them.

He turned with a barely concealed pride. "Hey, Evelyn, don't worry—"

At the look of shock streaking over her face he halted. Something behind him had caught her attention and he spun around.

He wasn't fast enough.

A large force crashed on top of him, roaring as it knocked him to his knees. His eyes traveled up, up, and up, to the figure of a large, dragon-like creature. It had the head of a lion and large, leathery wings that flapped fiercely against the sky as lightning flashed around the creature, highlighting its enormous size.

For a second he simply looked at it, estimating it was the size of at least eight men, then the creature opened its mouth, breaking his stunned paralysis. With seconds to spare, he rolled out of the way and scrambled inside the relative safety of the cave in time to avoid the blast of fire which shot out of the creature's open mouth.

"What the hell is that?"

He could hardly hear Evelyn's incredulous shouting over the noise of the monster but had no doubt about what stood in front of the cave.

Raising his voice, he yelled over the din the roaring beast was creating. "It's an *Umu nai'iru*, which literally translates to 'roaring weather-beast'. It's an ancient creature, one I'd always assumed to be a legend. They haven't been seen in thousands of years."

Evelyn gestured wildly in the direction of the creature with a combination of exasperation and bewilderment as Cat stirred behind her, no longer able to sleep due to the noise.

"It looks pretty freakin' real right now! What the hell are we supposed to do about it?"

Omar looked back to see the beast inhaling and flinched. It may have been too large to fit inside the cave, but it didn't need to get in. If it breathed fire into the cave, they were effectively, and literally, toast.

"We've got to lead it away, but I can't do it alone. It has both weather and earth magic and my power won't be enough. Maybe if we try together..."

Lightning flashed behind the creature but to his surprise, the creature roared and turned around.

This lightning isn't coming from the Umu nai'iru.

Wondering what else was out there but unable to see past the monster from where he stood, he moved further into the cave and closer to Cat and Evelyn.

He may not be able to defeat it, but he would protect them with his last breath if necessary.

Lightning stuck the ground right outside the cave as the unknown force battled with the *Umu nai'iru*. Whatever was casting the lightning wasn't on the creature's side, and from what he could tell, the fight didn't seem to be going well for the monster.

He edged back toward the mouth of the cave, unable to help himself. The clawed pedestal feet of the creature were now being lifted by a wind funnel, and it released a terrible howl, a noise far worse than the one which had first startled him.

A familiar voice came from nearby, surprising Omar with its soothing tone despite the situation.

"There, there, my lost one. No need to be so angry. It's time to go back where you belong. Worry not—it was cruel to bring you here like this and I shall avenge your pain."

The monster whimpered once before vanishing into the lightning splitting the sky.

Omar opened and closed his mouth helplessly as he attempted to process the amazing scene before him. "Robin? What..?"

Robin bounced into sight, smiling wide enough to reveal the dimples in both cheeks. "Hello there! I brought my friend, Aurora. We were in the neighborhood and thought we'd say hi."

Cat joined Omar at the mouth of the cave, making him start slightly. She smiled sheepishly at him before looking at Robin and Aurora, then gave a sweeping bow to the tall white eagle with a woman's face.

"Thanks for coming, Robin. You're always in the nick of time. Aurora, your presence is much appreciated."

Aurora inclined her head with a regal air. "You are most welcome. I have been searching for him for ages now. He was one of my creatures, but stolen away by the darkness centuries ago. I am most grateful to have him back. You may consider us even for this meeting. I have missed him most sorely."

Cat bowed her head. "I am in your debt, but will not argue if you feel this makes us even. Thank you again, Lady Aurora. I am at your command if you ever require my assistance."

Aurora nodded again before smiling at Robin. "Thank you for notifying me of this interesting development. I look forward to seeing you in the future."

Robin gave her his trademark bow, adding a flourish. "I am glad to be of aid, m'lady. We shall speak soon."

With that, the eagle-woman spread her wings, causing lightning to flash from her white feathers once more before she blasted into a sky that was dark as night with storm clouds. Once she was out of sight, the sky cleared rapidly, returning to the clear blue, sunny winter day it had been before.

With wide eyes, Omar turned to the women. "Wow. You know her?"

Cat nodded, but Evelyn shook her head.

"I've never seen her before. Robin, is this the 'old friend' you were talking about?"

Omar recognized the look on Evelyn's face. Almost simultaneously, he averted his eyes and pretended he hadn't seen it at all. A jealous woman wasn't someone he wanted to cross, especially not yet having witnessed Evelyn's full power for himself. He glanced at Cat, wondering if she could help, but she shook her head and stepped back.

"Let's stand over here," she whispered.

Omar nodded and they edged inside the cave together, leaving Robin and Evelyn to have some alone time. Whatever Robin said seemed to smooth things over, because when they rejoined them inside a few minutes later Evelyn was smiling again, and Robin was his usual carefree self.

"Everything okay?" Omar asked, hoping his face was neutral. He did not want to rock that particular boat.

"Why, of course!" Robin flashed a quick smile. "Aurora was in need of her creature and we were in need of someone who could trap the beast without injury. A win-win situation, as they say." He sobered, looking at each of them in turn. "The time is close. As Abbas grows stronger in the past, so too will the destructive magic grow in the present. We need to ensure the portal is prepared. We cannot do anything for Zahara on her end against him, but together, the four of us can ensure a safe landing place for her here."

Omar nodded as something tightened in his chest. "What do you need us to do?"

Instead of speaking, Robin handed each of them an object. To Omar, he gave a feather, Cat received a rock, and Evelyn was given a branch. Omar saw Robin kept a scarab beetle for himself.

"You must place this talisman over your heart, then in unison we shall repeat a prayer to help Zahara locate this place. Otherwise, she will become trapped in the in-between and never find her way home."

Omar gulped at the thought of Zahara being trapped forever. When he looked at Cat and Evelyn, he was relieved to see they wore expressions of fierce determination. He knew they would do anything for their friend.

"What's the prayer?" Cat was already holding her rock to her heart as she tilted her head, waiting for further instruction.

Evelyn moved her branch to the left side of her chest, and Omar placed his feather similarly. Robin nodded with satisfaction.

"Perfect. Now we can begin."

CHAPTER 21

Zahara crouched under the table, her small heart racing in fear. She recalled the time she'd held a rabbit in her hand. Its tiny body had quivered the same way; the poor heart had seemed like it would pop right out of the poor thing's chest. Looking back now, she felt bad for the rabbit, completely understanding how it felt for the first time as her own terror kept her frozen on the ground despite what her brain was telling her to do.

A cold swirl of air brushed her nose and she shivered as Abbas stepped slowly into the tent. His footsteps echoed against the soft carpet although she knew it shouldn't technically be possible.

"Where are you hiding, my foxy foe?"

He spoke calmly, but his deep voice sent shards of glass down her spine. She attempted to not hyperventilate in her hiding spot close to the ground, telling herself she could do it and trying to psych herself up to run or fight. But no matter what she did, she was unable to move, completely paralyzed by dread.

Reema stepped forward in the dim light, standing proudly in front of Abbas with her hair uncovered and her face shining with strength. Zahara's heart tried to leap out of her chest completely.

No!

"I am the one you are looking for."

"You?" Abbas tilted his head as he considered her claim, chuckling dryly before dismissing the idea. "No, I think...but no. You feel different, less...powerful. You are not the fox I am looking for."

Reema tilted her chin higher. "No, but I am the woman who started the feud between you and my husband. You murdered him for no reason other than your *pride*."

She spit the word at him like a profanity, but he brushed the accusation aside.

"Hardly. You are not worthy of my time. The prophecy needed Marwan for my destiny to be fulfilled. Now that," he growled, narrowing his eyes as he glared down at her, "is something to seek vengeance for."

"Prophecy?" Reema looked confused.

Zahara was confused as well, which somehow had the effect of relaxing her muscles enough to allow her to creep forward. The amulet dragged on the floor before she noticed and she paused, wondering if he'd heard the small scraping sound.

Abbas sneered. "I needed Marwan to control the empire. It spoke of his descendant controlling the magic in the Middle East. I planned to make that person my descendant, as well. I even went as far as lowering myself to beget a child on someone and letting the weakling live to ensure my destiny came true. Then your foolish husband went and 'fell in love.'" He laughed bitterly. "Love! Like love could ever be as valuable as true power! Love dies, but power lives on. Now it seems he has ruined my prophecy. I guess I will have to continue to grow my power the hard way."

Any semblance of amusement faded from his face as he stepped closer to Reema. His face was like granite, hard and immobile. "I shall kill you, the fox, and anything and anyone else who gets in my way to achieve my ultimate goal. I've already drained this land, but you and the fox should make a nice, light snack."

His hands sparked again with magic and Zahara saw it was the dark energy not the fire. She shouted a warning, then watched in horror as Reema's mother threw herself in front of her daughter, simultaneously pushing Reema away and into the corner where Haytham was tucked.

Reema screamed, tears pouring down her cheeks as the life drained from her mother's face. "*Umi!*"

Zahara's throat tightened at the thought of how she'd feel if it was her mum and the pain in her chest finally broke the last of her immobility. She sprang into action as Reema crumpled in the corner crying, trying to protect her son by holding him in her arms and shielding him from the dark jinn.

Zahara darted in front of them and bared her teeth. The fur on her neck was raised, and she knew this was it. The moment it all came down to.

"Finally." Abbas sighed, looking satisfied as he raised his hands. "I could feel your presence close by. I was wondering how many people I would have to kill to get your attention. I have to admit, I am rather disappointed. I was hoping I could kill them all while you watched, but I will return to take care of them later. You seem to be slightly more of a threat than a powerless woman and her baby."

Abbas closed his eyes and started to chant something in-comprehensible. Within seconds, the room began to spin around her and vertigo took over. The ground felt like it was dipping and lurching beneath her feet and the walls blinked in and out.

"What...what's happening?" She tried to focus her eyes, but couldn't.

It suddenly was like she was drunk. She tried to clear her head by shaking it, but it didn't work. Instead, it made her stumble.

Suddenly, Cat and Evelyn were in front of her.

Her eyes widened with hope. She stepped closer but stopped. Something was off. It was them, but they were too pale and still, lying completely motionless on the ground. When she saw the blood, her hand flew to her mouth and she almost fell down.

"Is this real?"

Something in the whisper of her own voice flipped a switch in her memory. She remembered someone saying this jinn could alter reality, but not that he could send her through time. He must be doing something to her, using some magic to make her see things that weren't real.

Concentrating on the ground and the power of the earth around her, she drew strength into herself and forced herself to focus beyond what she could see with her eyes.

An angry howl broke the connection. The image of her friends vanished as a small, brown bird began beating its wings against the jinn's head, clearing the last vestiges of her confu-sion. Abbas was distracted as he tried to swat the bird, and Reema leapt to her feet with a stick and joined in. The bird dove repeatedly, swooping in to pluck at any exposed flesh the stick wasn't hitting. Abbas roared with pain once more.

Zahara stood up and Reema screamed as she continued to hit Abbas with all her strength. "Go!"

Zahara didn't want to leave, but another loud voice shouted in her head and decided her course of action.

Zahara, it's time. You need to get to the portal, now, before it's too late.

MOVE!

Somehow she knew it was Evelyn, coming through loud and clear, and not just another illusion. Sending a prayer to all the gods she could recall, Zahara wished with all her heart for Reema and Haytham to be okay.

As she darted past them into the night, it struck her that the name Haytham meant 'hawk' in Arabic and wondered if it was the first time the baby had ever shifted.

ZAHARA FLEW PAST ROCKS and bushes, racing through the night on wings of fear and hope. Every thought was the same; the fear Abbas would kill them all, and the hope she'd make it to the portal before it was too late. The pain in her back legs made her wonder if they'd cramp up before she got there, but she pushed through.

Pain wasn't the worst thing awaiting her if she failed.

She halted, panting with effort by the time she'd reached the other side of the crevice, but she didn't pause long. She could see the vista stretching in front of her and anxiety gripped her tight. She still had to make it all the way back to the cave and the landscape looked different in the night.

What if she was going the wrong way? Her pace slowed as the pain in her legs mixed with indecision.

Which direction?

She could go forward or to the right. Trying to remember back to when Reema had first found her at the cave, Zahara closed her eyes, mentally retracing her steps. A small yip broke her concentration and she opened her eyes to see the red fox, staring at her with calm, wise vulpine eyes.

You again. I see you haven't died yet. Impressive.

Zahara tilted her head at his back-handed compliment.

Thank you. I have been lucky so far. But now I am being chased by the dark jinn who means to kill me and take away all that I hold dear. I need to get this amulet to the cave that brought me here. Can you help me again? I cannot offer you anything in exchange.

The red fox padded over, coming to the small alcove where she'd been stopped in indecision.

I know all too well the nature of this dark jinn. He is cruel and sends dogs to destroy all living things he does not feel are worthy of destruction at his own hand. I do not like him, nor have any loyalty to his cause. I will show you the way simply because I no longer wish him to blight my land. Be warned, however, that I cannot stop him if he reaches you.

The fox's tail flicked as it spoke, and Zahara nodded. It was a fair deal.

Your help is much appreciated. I understand. You must protect your family as well.

The fox nodded once then turned and began to run. Zahara followed, impressed by its speed. She could run faster, but only because she had magic to give her an extra boost. As far as she could tell, the red fox had no magic except for the strength of heart required to help in the face of a magic they both despised.

As a consequence, the twenty-minute walk became a five minute run. When Zahara saw the cave looming in front of them, relief washed over her in a giant wave.

I cannot thank you enough. May Allah and the earth bless you and your family.

The red fox gave her a lingering look.

Take care, Zahara of the Earth. I will hope for your success.

Even as the fox thought the words, it was gone, bounding off into the night. Soon, it had disappeared entirely from view and she realized with a sense of bemusement they'd never exchanged names.

As she turned to walk to the cave, she couldn't help but wonder how the fox had known who she was but was grateful they had. Perhaps one day she'd ask Robin. Hopefully, she'd get the chance.

Zahara sniffed for danger as she padded across the threshold of the cave. Smelling nothing but sand and the desert night air, she entered with cautious steps, looking around for the place she needed to stand.

It was the same cave she'd arrived in Reema's time in, and nothing had changed as far as she could see. It was still dead, with no magic anywhere. There was no portal, real or supernatural, leading anywhere. The only way in or out of the cave was the way she'd entered. Frustrated and sore, she let out a sigh of despair and rested her head on her paws, closing her eyes and sending out a silent prayer.

Someone, please help me. I have the amulet. I'm in the place I was supposed to be, but I need help. I don't know how to get home from here. If anyone is listening, I could really use a hand.

But instead of the kind voice of the fox or a light shining on the wall with an exit sign, the dark voice Zahara had hoped never to hear again answered her silent request.

"So, you have decided this is the location you wish to have your burial? A fitting place, really. At least you will have the company of another soldier."

Zahara's head jerked up from her paws as she whirled to face Abbas, seeing a faint flickering shadow shaped like a man waver behind him. She got an overwhelming feeling of sadness as the figure of a ghost winked out.

During the brief distraction, Abbas had continued to walk toward her, dark and majestic with his robes swirling from a wind he seemed to be generating all by himself. He laughed coldly and taunted her further, causing the fur on her neck to rise.

"Oh, and your friends are dead if you were curious. I made short work of them after you left. A baby hawk and a woman are hardly a challenge."

He pretended to dust his hands off when tears welled in her eyes.

Zahara stumbled, almost collapsing from the weight of her grief until she remembered something. "Oh, you did? That's too bad. They made good food."

She listened to the words coming out of her mouth and was amazed by her bravado. She sounded so steady and heartless. Maybe some of Vanessa's advice on acting was paying off, because he seemed to buy it.

Abbas paused to stare at her, eyebrows wrinkling before his face smoothed out into his usual evil expression. "Well, I had hoped to hurt you with their deaths but it appears they were not as important to you as I had thought. No matter. All I require is the amulet. I believe it shall be a wonderful addition for aiding in my consolidation of power. It smells of strong magic. I'll take it from you now."

Zahara's large ears folded back against her head. She bared her teeth. "No, you won't. Not over my dead body."

Abbas chuckled and without waiting, formed another ball in his hands. "Oh, yes I will."

This ball was different from the fire balls and the black ones he'd thrown before, appearing to be formed of ice. She jumped to the side before she could examine it fully but wasn't fast enough. The ball splintered when it hit the wall, ricocheting pieces all around the cave.

One caught her front paw, and as the cold shard drove into the soft pad, she howled in pain. Backing away, she held it up to look and saw she was bleeding heavily. Whimpering, she took a quick swipe at it with her tongue before she glared at him.

"You won't win. I won't stop trying to defeat you, as long as I have breath in my body."

Panting from pain and exertion, she searched desperately for the portal, but all she saw was the cave.

Where is it?

She was stuck in a cave with her back literally against the wall, with a powerful amulet she didn't know how to use and an evil jinn facing her who had just told her he'd murdered her ancestors and was now threatening to murder her, plus or minus a few ghosts.

I could really use a hand right now. Someone? Anyone?

She realized she'd backed herself into a corner and watched helplessly as Abbas continued his slow approach. She was bleeding, her paw was excruciatingly painful, and she couldn't concentrate enough to use her earth power. Unable to focus, her magic seemed to have deserted her entirely. Closing her eyes, she wondered if it would hurt to die.

Abbas looked gleeful when she opened her eyes. He had stopped only a few paces away as he smirked down at her, gloating over her trembling form.

"Poor little fox. Thought your power was enough to defeat me, did you? Poor, stupid bitch."

Zahara's head snapped up at his words. The fire of anger replaced her hopeless fear and gave her strength as she stretched to her full fox height. Standing her ground on injured and painful paws, she bared her teeth again.

"Don't. Call. Me. A. Bitch!" Her power rose as she spat the words, then closed her eyes and called to the dirt and rocks in the cave and felt them answer.

The ground began to rumble, letting out a deep groan from somewhere far below as the earth shifted. Abbas stepped back, eyebrows raised with concern as he scanned the cave.

"What are you doing? Stop it!"

Zahara let a laugh bubble out. *My turn.* "Oh, you don't like that? I may not be able to win, but at least I can cause you pain. I don't care if I walk away from this, but I'll make sure you don't either."

She concentrated on the rocks which made up the land, calling them to come and rearrange themselves. Cracks began to appear in the floor and rocks fell from the ceiling.

"Stop it! You're going to collapse the cave. We'll be trapped here!"

Zahara opened her eyes and smiled, letting her tongue loll out. "I know. That's the point. If I can't kill you, I'll make sure you are buried deep in the earth forever."

Abbas screamed, forming another black ball in his hands as Zahara hit him with a rock from the ceiling.

In the midst of all the shaking, rocks falling around them, and noise, her amulet began to glow a bright, emerald green.

CHAPTER 22

O mar repeated the words Robin had bid them to say, clutching the talisman closer to his heart with each repetition.

Zahara, come home, please.

When he opened his eyes, each object was glowing a different color. The branch was green, the feather purple, the rock was a soft blue, and the beetle Robin had kept for himself had become a fiery red. As they began another round of chanting, the center of the circle begin to glow a brilliant green and his eyes widened. When the green began to fade, he realized he'd stopped chanting. Hurrying to continue, he spoke the words with more ferocity now he could see something happening.

Zahara, we're here for you.

With an unexpectedly loud bang, accompanied by a wind that knocked them all over, Zahara appeared. He was the first to regain his footing, but what he saw horrified him. He'd never seen Zahara as a fox before but knew it was her. It was the condition she was in which had thrown him.

The small fox held up one front paw, dripping with blood. Her flanks were covered with brambles and more blood, and she appeared to be literally on her last leg of energy as she limped forward. Before he could act, the fox yipped and moved back and out of the circle.

"What is it?" Cat's words were hardly audible as the noise of the wind increased.

Omar would have thought the wind should have diminished if Zahara had successfully returned through the portal but as she backed away from the still-glowing doorway, he heard her frantic response.

"He's coming! He's right behind me. We have to stop him from coming through!"

Fear shone in the small face as the fox turned to face the portal.

Robin stood and began to chant something inaudible over the sound of the raging wind as a dark arm began to emerge from the doorway. At the sight of the arm he yelled, this time loudly enough to be heard above the din.

"Zahara, use the amulet. *Now*!"

Zahara shook her head, tears welling in her eyes. "I don't know how!"

Robin gestured impatiently at the necklace. "Tell it to close the door!"

Omar realized he'd never heard Robin shout before when Zahara nodded, closing her eyes. The green from the amulet grew stronger. The light spread until it was large enough to encompass Zahara with its power. Then, as if a door had been slammed shut, the portal winked out.

A single, blood-curdling scream bounced off the walls of the cave as the wind abruptly ceased and the cave fell silent. An instant later, Zahara crumpled to the ground. Omar rushed to her side to find the small fox laying on the floor, a dull green necklace around her neck and a single dark, cloth covered arm on the ground beside her.

THE NEXT TIME ZAHARA opened her eyes, she was looking into a clear, blue sky. Clouds scuttled lazily across the giant canvas above her as she stared up at it, and it took a moment for the events to come crashing back in.

Her body felt surprisingly good, as though nothing had ever happened to her, and she looked at her hand, clenching and unclenching it with wonder.

It was perfect.

She remembered the last thing she'd seen and bolted upright, whipping her head around as fear rose in her chest and stole her breath.

A soft male voice came from somewhere just behind her. "Hey, calm down. Everything is okay."

When she turned, she saw Omar beside her, watching her with a worried expression. She realized she was lying on a blanket beside the Jeep, with the hard metal surface of the vehicle at her back and Cat and Evelyn a few feet away talking softly to each other.

Once she verified everything around her was safe, some of her tension eased and she gazed up at him, shyness replacing her waking terror. "What happened?"

The words came out like a croak and she winced. She tried to clear her dry throat, gratefully accepting his offer of a water bottle and drinking half with a greedy joy before handing it back with a relieved sigh.

"Thank you. I needed that."

He smiled with a warmth that caused her cheeks to glow. Something about the way he watched her reminded her of how she'd seen Jake look at Mai, or how Robin looked at Evelyn. Her eyes widened.

Could he, did he have feelings for her?

Suddenly, all of the trauma she'd been through faded and she looked down, unable to process this one new idea on the heels of everything else. She realized he was speaking and made a concentrated effort to focus on his words. It was hard not to wonder what his smile meant but once she was able to understand what he was saying, she sobered instantly.

"When you came through the portal, Abbas followed. Somehow, you managed to close the portal despite him being there. Robin says you used the amulet's spell the way Marwan had intended all along."

"What does that mean?"

She felt stupid, but wasn't sure if it was from exhaustion or because she'd lost brain cells from all the magic she'd been drenched in. Whatever the cause, what he was trying to say still wasn't computing.

"It means you did it, Zahara." His smile grew. "You stopped Abbas. For good. He's trapped inside the portal and can't get out, ever."

"For the next million years anyway." Satisfaction coursed through Zahara when she remembered the exact wording of the spell she'd cast. She frowned as something occurred to her. "But wait—Abbas said he killed Reema and Haytham. I failed."

Omar shook his head. "No, he didn't. If he had, you wouldn't be here, remember?"

Zahara nodded. She'd been sure of that while she'd been fighting Abbas but was glad to have confirmation now her thoughts were so confused. Maybe portal travel was hard on the brain? Like, not enough oxygen during the hundreds of years of transport?

It was worse than a hangover.

"If he didn't kill them, what happened? That was several hundred years ago. If I'm back here, I'll never see them again. I'll never know if they were okay."

Conflicting waves of sadness and elation washed through her. She realized even though she'd succeeded in removing the threat to her family, she'd still lost something precious. On one hand, she'd done what she'd been tasked to do and had completed her quest. The amulet had been successfully returned to Petra when it was needed, and her ancestors and entire family were safe from the evil jinn because he was trapped for a million years in the portal.

But she'd also watched Marwan die, seen Reema's mother make the ultimate sacrifice to save her daughter and grandson, and faced down evil alone, almost dying herself in the process. Her eyes welled as emotion overflowed.

"They died protecting each other."

She couldn't hold back her grief any longer. Tears streamed down her face and her shoulders shook as she cried, but she wasn't alone. Warm arms encircled her, guiding her head to a strong shoulder with as much as care as if she was made out of glass, and a wide hand gently rubbed her back.

"Shhh, *habibi*. It's okay. You're home now. I'm here, if you need me, and your friends are here, too. There is no greater honor than to die protecting your family and we would all give our lives for you."

Zahara hardly heard the words he murmured into her hair but as they began to sink in, her sadness gave way to a sense of peace. He was right. She was home.

Lifting her head off his shoulder, she stared into deep brown eyes, which swirled with feeling. She looked into them for what felt like eternity as he slowly lowered his head.

She closed her eyes as he took her lips with a gentleness that brought another round of tears. The same glorious tingle she'd felt in his presence before she'd fallen into the past overwhelmed her, along with the knowledge that at last, she was falling into her future.

CHAPTER 23

"Um, hey." Cat cleared her throat. "I hope we're not interrupting."

Cat and Evelyn had waited until Zahara and Omar finished speaking before they came back to the Jeep, but Zahara blushed anyway, knowing they'd been close enough to see what their 'talking' had involved.

"No, not at all. Omar was filling me in on what happened while I was away."

Zahara hated the fact her face was a fiery red under its normal tan but couldn't help it. She figured Cat would understand as she was red more often than not, but she didn't know how she was supposed to act now. She glanced shyly at Omar, finding him watching her with a warm and loving look, and a small smile crept over her lips.

Evelyn smirked and raised an eyebrow. "Filling you in, was he?"

Zahara laughed. "Yes, okay. Fine. He filled me in and may have mentioned wanting to spend time with me. Happy now?"

Evelyn smiled, the warmth encompassing both Zahara and Omar. "Very. It's the best news I've heard all week."

Evelyn and Cat both gave Zahara a big hug, then Cat gestured to her body.

"We're glad you made it back in one piece. I hope you don't mind, but I took the liberty of doing a little healing for you. Nothing was broken, but you were pretty banged up and had some deep puncture wounds. Of course, I might have accidentally finished the rest of Omar's food in the process of recovering, so we'll have to go back to Wadi Musa to buy more if you're hungry." Cat shot Omar a look of gratitude mixed with embarrassment. "Thanks again, and I really am sorry I didn't share."

He waved her apology away. "I'm glad you were able to heal Zahara. I'm pretty sure it was the blood loss which caused her to pass out when she returned." He looked at Zahara, his expression solemn. "I don't know what happened to your paw, but I could see bone, and you were bleeding profusely when you came through the portal."

"Robin said your blood was the reason you were able to open the portal in the first place." Evelyn spoke up.

Zahara turned to her, raising her eyebrows. "Really? My bleeding paw was the reason the spell worked?"

Evelyn nodded. "Yes, between your blood and the magic you were spilling, Robin said you were the reason everything was shaking. You were on the verge of creating another earthquake as big as the one that originally destroyed the magic here when you came through. Luckily that didn't happen, or you would have destroyed the cave and the portal to boot. Double lucky, because it provided the exact combo of magic and blood needed to punch the door to our time open from your end, and kept it open long enough to use the amulet's spell to trap Abbas."

Zahara flexed her now intact hand. "I had no idea. I was so mad at Abbas I didn't care if I lived or died. I just knew there was no way I was going to give him the satisfaction of winning. I wasn't sure he hadn't killed Reema and Haytham at the time, but the thought of keeping them safe motivated me as well."

Cat shuddered, giving her a sympathetic look. "I can imagine how awful that must have been. I still remember how I felt when my mom and dad ended up in hospital because someone was after me. It's an awful feeling."

Zahara didn't know Cat's parents, but knew the McLeans were a close knit family like hers. She remembered the look on Reema's face when her mum had thrown herself in front of her and taken the blast of dark magic. Love and anguish beyond belief.

I'm so glad my parents and brothers are safe thousands of miles away from here.

Evelyn patted Cat's shoulder. "It was pretty awful. But everything worked out in the end." She looked at Zahara. "It's over here too. Robin finally came through—he even brought help! Aurora, the eagle-goddess who trained Vanessa, showed up to take care of a pretty scary desert-dragon-monster before you came back. And Robin helped us get the portal ready."

Cat shook her head with amazement. "Yeah, he really came through. I've known him for years and this is the first time he's taken real action as opposed to just spouting cryptic messages. I'm not sure what you were up against, but it must have been huge for him to feel the need to step in. And you did it alone on your end, which is even more impressive."

Zahara looked down, remembering the way her ancestors had fought to live. Her voice was quiet when she spoke. "I didn't do it alone. I had so much help. Marwan died protecting us while we mixed the spell. I even had a red fox, an ordinary animal, guide me where I needed to go, twice. And I had Reema and her *umi* helping me." Zahara's eyes welled again, remembering the last time she'd seen them. "Reema's mum died protecting her and the baby, Haytham."

She wiped her eyes, and a watery chuckle escaped as she remembered the child who'd been at the center of it all.

"He turned into a hawk and tore the crap out of Abbas' face. Looking back, it was kind of funny. So no, I most definitely wasn't alone back there. And of course, I had you guys on this end."

Evelyn shrugged. "Say what you will, you deserve major props. You proved stubborn can get you through even the darkest night. I'm proud of you, Z."

Zahara smiled, not deflecting the praise this time. "Well, yes, stubborn *will* take you places, that I will not deny. If you ask my parents, they'll tell you I have a habit of doing things the hard way because I'm a little *too* stubborn. Hey, speaking of places, I'm hungry. Cat said she ate all our food, so can we go somewhere and get more?"

Cat and Evelyn laughed, then each took an arm and helped Zahara to her feet. Omar gave her another secret smile before lightly touching her hand.

"In that case, let's get in the Jeep. We'll stay in Wadi Musa tonight and start back to the gate tomorrow."

Cat sighed, patting her stomach. "That sounds lovely. Food, shower, then home. I've enjoyed every minute of this trip—well, not *every* minute— but I do need to get back to school."

Evelyn nodded. "Me too. Well, not school, but I've got other business to attend to. I'm good with an itinerary of eat, sleep, and travel."

Zahara smiled. Now that the terror of her unexpected trip into the past was over, things felt brighter than ever. As she took one last look around the rocky land before getting into the vehicle, she sensed magic all around her. Touching the now-quiet amulet on her chest, her smile grew.

She'd done it.

She'd brought the amulet to Petra and saved her family, and even returned magic to a place that had been without for centuries.

That was *definitely* worth a few burgers.

ZAHARA LEANED BACK in her chair. Two burgers had been enough to sate her appetite, and now she was enjoying the interaction between Omar and her friends. They were treating him exactly how she treated her brothers. They'd been through a lot together trying to get her home, and the connection it had forged showed.

Omar had taken them to a nice restaurant close to the hotel, where they proceeded to devour enough food for a caravan of ten men. She'd watched with amusement as his eyes had gotten wider as Cat finished off triple helpings of everything.

Cat blushed when she'd noticed his awe. "What? I get hungry when I use my powers."

Omar held up his hands protectively. "I completely understand, it's just, well, I've been around a while now and I've never seen anyone eat like this before."

Evelyn elbowed him. "You should see her and her sister in action together. Now *that's* impressive. With or without magic, those two girls can pack it away."

Overcome with love, Zahara smiled. *They are my warriors and my family.*

"I'm going to miss you guys," she blurted.

"We'll miss you too, Zahara, but we'll see you again soon." Cat gave her a quizzical look around her fourth— or was it her fifth?—burger.

She smiled, knowing Cat was trying to read her aura by the way her eyes had become unfocused. When Cat continued to observe her, Zahara shook her head.

"I know, it's just...you're so far away. It was great having this week together. Well, mostly together. I wish we all lived in the same tiny village and could see each other every day."

"Oh, that would be great," Cat agreed. "Could you imagine? If everyone you loved all lived in the same block or town? That way you'd always be close to them and never have to miss anyone." She paused. "Hmm, on second thought that may be too much commitment. I need my space too."

Evelyn laughed. "Oh, my little introvert. Don't worry, in our imaginary village you get a safe room where you can read alone at all times of the day whenever you need to be by yourself, okay? We'll call it the Cat Cave."

Cat took another bite from her burger and chewed while she thought. "Deal."

Omar cleared his throat. "There's one more thing we need to do before we head back to Summerland."

Zahara frowned. "What's that?"

Omar glanced around to ensure they were alone, then leaned forward and dropped his voice. "Robin wants us to meet him tonight, back at the treasury. He didn't say why, but did say it was important. He had to leave before you woke up, Zahara, but wanted a word with you before you went home."

Zahara's eyebrows raised. Robin wanted to talk to her? Before they went home? She wasn't sure why Omar's words made her nervous. She'd talked to Robin loads of times in the past without fear. But something about his quiet words now sent a tingle of foreboding through her.

"Do I have time for a shower and a nap first?" Zahara looked down at her dirty and ripped clothing.

None of them had taken the time to change before eating. With Zahara and Cat ready to eat a camel, Omar had assured them they looked fine. As long as they were fully covered, dirt wouldn't bother most people living in the middle of the desert.

"Of course. I will come knock on your door at ten tonight. That will give you close to six hours to rest and clean up."

Zahara sighed. Her body was tired enough to sleep for days, but her curiosity about what Robin wanted to talk to her about made her wonder if she'd be able to relax enough to sleep at all.

CHAPTER 24

Zahara was surprised to discover she'd succeeded in falling asleep when a light tap on the door woke her. The last time she'd looked at the clock it had been just after five. Apparently in spite of her concerns, her body's needs had overruled her mind's usually endless ability to spin in circles.

She stretched in the bed, gloriously limber after the memory of the pain, which had been in almost every part of her body only a few hours earlier. She was so grateful she had a friend like Cat who could heal anything barring death.

Zahara padded to the door in her comfortable cotton pjs and opened it with a yawn. Rubbing her eyes as her hair spilled over her back and shoulders, she lowered her hand and blinked into Omar's surprised face.

"Oh, hello. Do you want to come in?" When he blushed and began to turn around, she touched his arm to stop him. "Please, we're dressed, mostly. You don't have to wait in the hallway like room service."

Omar shook his head, giving her a crooked smile. "I don't feel like a servant, Zahara, but I'm not ready to see you like this. Not with your friends here. You're far too beautiful for me to see you in your night clothes, even if you are completely covered."

It was her turn to blush. Her hands went to her face to try to cool down the burning. "Omar, I totally forgot. I'm sorry. I'll get dressed and make sure we're ready in two minutes."

Omar smiled and before she could disappear to hide her mortification, he leaned forward to brush a lock of hair off her face. Staring into her eyes with a warmth promising more, his lip quirked up.

"Believe me, you have nothing to apologize for. Take your time. I will wait for you as long as you need me to."

Zahara nodded, breathless and pretty sure there were stars in her eyes when she gently closed the door on his handsome face. Once he was out of sight, she took a deep breath and closed her eyes for a second, then grabbed her clothes and hurried to change.

Once Cat and Evelyn were ready, they opened the door to find Omar leaning on the wall, scrolling on his phone.

He looked up and smiled, putting his phone away before pointing at their backpacks with a raised eyebrow. "You ready for home?"

"We figured we'd pack all of our stuff now. You never know what's going to happen with Robin," Cat replied, shrugging her backpack on.

"Better safe than sorry," Evelyn agreed. "After all, if Robin can make it here, chances are good he can send us home whenever he wants as well."

He laughed. "Very true. I never know what to expect with Robin. Now, remember to remain quiet. There is an unofficial curfew here, and we don't want to draw extra attention."

They followed him to the car, remaining silent after his warning. The night was clear and calm and the stars seemed close enough to touch. Zahara soaked in the beauty of the desert as they drove, watching the scenery pass in awe. By the time they arrived in Petra, she was invigorated by the chill. Even though they had to park further away this time, the walk to the treasury was an easy stroll.

It looks so different at night.

Zahara gazed up at the facade of the treasury in front of her, trying to imagine how hard it would have been to carve something so grand into a sheet of rock at the time it had been accomplished. She was in awe of the ingenuity of people.

They waited in the dark for several minutes before the sound of someone approaching caught her attention. Her nerves uncomfortably tight, she turned to see who was there. So far on this trip, approaching footsteps hadn't been a good thing.

Relief filled her when she saw Robin, even though he looked more solemn than usual. He stood tall in the form of a young man, and while objectively quite handsome, she missed the cute eight-year-old she was used to playing with in the meadows back home.

"Hello, ladies. Omar." Robin nodded before unceremoniously plopping down into a cross-legged position near a boulder. "I am glad you were able to come tonight. I wanted to speak with you before you return to your homes."

Cat bowed her head slightly before sitting beside him. "Thank you, Robin. I'm always honored to have any of your time."

Evelyn knelt beside Robin, bestowing a light kiss on his lips. "And you know I'm always happy to see you."

Omar bowed as well, sitting across from Robin. "Old friend, it is a pleasure. Thank you. For everything."

Robin gave them an inclusive smile before letting his gaze rest upon Zahara. "I needed to speak with you before you return home."

Zahara's heart rate picked up. "I'm listening."

Robin bit his lip then sighed. "It is difficult to explain. This story is much older than you are and too complicated to be laid out smoothly. You already know some of it. You found Abbas and defeated him with the amulet you were sent in the mail. Your Aunt Reema was no longer able to protect it, which was why it was sent to you in the first place."

Zahara nodded. "My mum told me it was for one of us to take. I chose to protect it because my brothers had other commitments."

Robin shook his head. "No, this was always meant to be your quest. It was never for any male descendant to accomplish. While you may have grown up fighting your brothers for supremacy, you were always the one destined to save your family."

Zahara's eyes prickled with tears at his unexpected words. "But why me?"

Robin bobbed his head, looking earnest. "This is where the prophecy becomes tricky. You see, Abbas knew the prophecy about Marwan's descendant inheriting the power of the earth in the Middle East. He wanted to tap into the power and assumed by marrying a child of his own flesh and blood to Marwan that the prophecy could be controlled by him. But he was wrong."

"I know he didn't succeed, but how does this relate to me specifically?"

He smiled and dropped his voice into the storyteller cadence she'd always loved so much. "Let me tell you a tale of prophecy and magic. Once upon a time, the world was a place full of magic and danger. People hid from that which they didn't understand. They made settlements for protection and for companionship. They had children and families and spread across the land. Magic was something they believed in, but also something to be feared and desired. Some creatures were able to coexist peacefully with humans; others could not, or did not wish to. The jinn were similar in many ways to humans and began to mingle with them. They had magic, but their numbers were smaller. Soon they began to intermarry, passing the magic along, which created a new community with traits of both groups. Some jinn felt this was beneath them however, and believed humans should be used only as servants or slaves."

Zahara thought about his words. She could believe Abbas had been a jinn who saw humans as slaves to control. "That makes sense. How does Abbas play into this?"

Robin tilted his head. "Abbas came into the world several millennia before you did. He was a powerful jinn and when he saw other jinn being captured, even used by humans as a wish-delivery device, he became enraged. He vowed he would control the entire world and subject the inferior humans to the same yokes jinn had been subjecteded to. Using his magic, he caused the earthquake here and succeeded in draining the land of its magic in order to bolster his own. If it had not been for the most human of emotions, he likely would have succeeded with his plans and gained the domination he craved."

Cat nodded. "Love?"

Robin smiled. "Yes, Cat, love. Marwan had already promised to marry Abbas's daughter when he met Zahara's ancestor by chance in the marketplace one day. Their souls called to each other at first sight. Before Abbas could stop them, Marwan disappeared into the desert with Reema. Together they had a son, Haytham."

Robin looked at Zahara, nodding. "You've met him. As you saw, he inherited his father's magic and his mother's human persistence and strength. And because of some 'divine' intervention, Reema and Haytham were able to escape from his clutches and continue your family line."

He winked and she wondered if he meant himself when he said 'divine', but he still hadn't answered her question.

She shook her head. "Why was it so important *I* was the one to return the amulet?"

Robin's eyes twinkled. "As it so often occurs, the prophecy was misinterpreted. It was never Marwan's son who was supposed to control the power here, the way Abbas had assumed. It was his descendant who was prophesied, but there was never any mention of Marwan's child. The original prophecy tells of a descendant blessed by foxes, with their cunning and fortitude as well as the magic of earth."

Zahara's breath left in a whoosh. "The red fox?"

Robin chuckled. "An old friend."

Zahara sat back, stunned. "So, all this time, it was supposed to happen this way? I was always going to receive the amulet and go back to help?"

Robin tilted his head. "In some form or another, this was always your battle. The amulet has now been returned and recharged."

Zahara looked at the amulet she had worn around her neck since the first time she'd put it on in the cave. She felt naked without it now, even more so since her return to the present. Somehow, its warmth against her chest made her feel more whole.

"The amulet belongs here, Zahara." Robin's face was solemn.

"But..." Zahara started to protest but stopped when she looked into his eyes, reading the truth. "I see." She looked at the amulet again. "I'm meant to stay here as well, aren't I?"

He nodded. "Yes, Zahara. You are needed here. *I* need you here, to keep the magic alive in the land. It has been struggling for so long, limping by with little outside help. While I am impressive, I am only one god and cannot be everywhere at once. You must nurture the magic of this land while I protect mine."

Zahara looked at her friends. They'd been listening with mixed expressions of sadness and acceptance. When she looked at Omar, his face shone with a tentative hope that made her spirit rise. Maybe if she was meant to be here, they were meant to be together as well.

Suddenly, moving didn't sound so bad.

She stood up, brushing her slacks off. "I understand. It's time for me to take up my duties here. But what about Cat and Evelyn?"

Robin stood and held out his hands, and when she accepted, he gave them a light squeeze. "I shall take them home. It will be a quicker journey than usual, but I think they can handle it now that they have their own powers to protect them."

He dropped her hands, pulling her into an unexpectedly tight hug. She melted into his arms as memories of her childhood with him flashed through her mind. He'd always been there for her, training her, encouraging her to practice. So much made sense now that hadn't before.

Zahara stepped back, giving him a wistful look. "Will I see you again?"

"Of course you will, my little fox! I am a god of the earth, after all! There's nowhere on the planet I can't go."

Zahara smiled, relief she wouldn't be without her mentor adding to her gratitude. "Thank you for everything, Robin. You know, I always wondered what my purpose was. I felt so restless growing up, not like my brothers, who always seemed to have a plan. I think maybe some part of me always knew there was something else, something *more* I was supposed to be doing. I finally feel like I'm ready to take my place in the world."

"You're welcome, my child. Cat? Evelyn, my love? Are you ladies ready to travel?"

Cat and Evelyn took turns hugging Zahara.

"You be safe, okay?" Cat whispered, kissing her on the cheek. "Don't forget to text!"

Zahara smiled. "I promise."

"That goes ditto for me, got it?" Evelyn gave her a stern look that morphed into a second hug at her nod of agreement.

"I'll miss you guys. Thanks. For everything."

Cat and Evelyn waved then took the hands Robin held out to them. In a flash, they were gone, leaving Omar and Zahara alone beside the ancient treasury in a star-filled desert night.

CHAPTER 25

S ilence fell like a blanket between them and Zahara realized it was the first time she'd been alone with Omar. It was the middle of the night and Petra felt different now. It was nice they hadn't had to gate her friends back after a long drive, but it left her feeling somehow adrift.

Zahara turned to Omar. "Now what?"

As the words fell between them, they watched each other. She was a stranger in a strange land with a man she barely knew, yet felt oddly at home. Well, except for the part where she had no idea what she was supposed to do next.

Omar shrugged before looking up into the starry sky. "We could lay down and count the stars. Are you in a rush?"

Zahara laughed. It was an unexpected answer but sounded like a wonderful idea. "I'd like that."

At her reply, he flashed a smile and grabbed his trusty picnic blanket from the back of the Jeep. They'd eaten on it a few times since starting her quest, but it looked comfortable in the dark in a way it hadn't before. After he carefully smoothed it out, she sat on the edge with a strange shyness as she waited for him to sit beside her. When he lay down, Zahara followed suit, and soon they were both looking up at the stars, close but not quite touching.

"When I was a child, the stars looked like this everywhere. There were only a few large cities competing with them for brightness and even then, nighttime was mostly dark until electricity became common." He sighed wistfully, falling silent again.

Zahara turned her head to the left to look at his profile. He was still looking up, which allowed her a chance to watch him unobserved. He looked sad and she remembered for the first time since returning how old he was. Life would have changed so much over the last century.

"It must have been interesting, growing up during such turbulent times," she said, finally settling on a platitude. How did she ask about his past, with everything he must have gained and lost?

"Interesting is one way of putting it," he chuckled. "I was here for the discovery of electricity, cars, planes, the Internet." He shook his head, turning abruptly to catch her staring at him.

Zahara knew her cheeks were flushed but hoped the night hid her reaction to the way he looked at her. His lips were only a few inches away. Was he going to kiss her?

"And yet with everything I've seen, I've never met anyone as special as you."

Her eyes prickled unexpectedly. How did he do that? He made her feel more important than anything or anyone else. Even fighting and defeating Abbas didn't feel as magical or powerful to her as this moment with him.

"I've...never met anyone like you, either."

Her whispered words seemed to galvanize him. He leaned closer and the distance between them vanished.

At first, the kiss was as gentle as the one earlier. The light touch of lips against lips was like silk brushing against electric silk. But within seconds, Zahara's skin felt too tight, bursting with heat as the kiss deepened.

His arms went around her, and she lost herself in the warm cocoon of his embrace for an eternity in the dark night. She wouldn't have been surprised to discover a hundred years had passed in the time she was there. Then slowly, reluctantly, he pulled back.

He rested his forehead on hers and she felt his soft breath on her face before he settled back with her in his arms. With Zahara tucked into the nook between his arm and chest, she closed her eyes and felt her heart race in unison with his.

"Now what?" Zahara whispered the words again, but this time, they had a different meaning.

Before, she'd wondered what she was supposed to do, but now she was really asking what would happen between them. With all their responsibilities, could they have a future together? The future seemed wide open but clouded, and she couldn't see a path through her confusion.

Omar sighed, pulling her tighter to her chest. "Before anything else happens between us, Robin asked me to do one more thing."

She pulled back, her surprise causing her to sit up. She shivered in the cool night, instantly missing the warmth of his arms. "What? I thought everything was over."

Omar sat up, turning to watch her as he took her hands in his. "Yes and no. You've done everything you needed to do to defeat Abbas, that part is done. You've recharged the amulet and Robin has asked you to stay and protect the magic here. So, the initial hard work is finished."

"But?" Zahara heard it coming the second he said 'initial'.

"But, according to Robin, we need to visit one of your relatives to truly finish things. Their house is on the way to Shobak. I was going to take you there tomorrow, once you were more rested." Omar looked like a little boy who'd been caught stealing cookies. "I hope you aren't upset I didn't say anything earlier. I was distracted by the stars, and your eyes."

Zahara could hear his honesty as he waited with an anxious look on his face. Suddenly, she couldn't help smiling. "I've never sat on a blanket under the stars with anyone before. I'm glad I had a chance to do this first, before getting back to work. It's so beautiful here."

He drew her back in for a hug before slowly letting go. "As much as I enjoy being here with you, I don't think I'll succeed in being a gentleman if we stay much longer. But before we go, I'd love a chance to run with you in the moonlight." He stood, throwing her a wink. "Are you up for a romp?"

Zahara stood as he transformed in a blur of fur and her heart leapt. She'd known he had powers, but not that he could become a red fox. She thought back to the fox who'd helped her so long ago and yet so recently.

Could it be? He'd said his family had been here for ages, but she'd thought that fox had been a simple, earthly creature. *Was it possible?*

Brushing aside the sudden surplus of questions for the time being, she transformed as well. At the moment, she needed to run more than she needed answers. Seconds later, two small foxes raced off into the bright, star-filled night through the ancient Nabatean kingdom, rulers of everything the light touched.

ZAHARA GROANED AS SHE opened her eyes to the blinding sunlight. She would absolutely never get used to cheap hotel blinds. One minute she'd was sleeping comfortably; the next minute the sun was stabbing her through the retinas because of a cheap Venetian knock-off.

As the memory of the previous night flashed through her mind, her irritation faded. It had been an amazing night. She sighed, remembering both the romance and the fun. She hadn't been on many first dates, and the handful she had been on hadn't been worth writing home about. Zero percent of those had led her to looking forward to a second.

Last night completely broke that mold.

While she'd worked hard to hide any hint of a romantic side from her brothers to avoid their incessant teasing, last night had fulfilled every single one of those silly romantic fantasies. It had been more than just the star-gazing and wonderful kiss, though she was pretty sure she could pull that memory out and sigh for a long time. What had really captured her heart was when he'd challenged her inner fox to run and play.

And they had, almost until dawn.

It had been amazing to see Petra by night, without throngs of tourists obstructing her view of the magnificent caves and architecture. They'd zipped through narrow passages carved by wind and water, darted through small burrows she'd never have been able to find as a person, and climbed to the top of several of the structures to sit and look at the landscape from a bird's eye view.

A smile curved her lips as she marveled at how lucky she was. She had no idea where things would lead with Omar, but after last night, she couldn't wait to find out. Only one more stop until she had a chance to explore their connection further.

With excitement now powering her movements, she dressed and repacked with more speed than usual. The room felt empty without her friends and a twinge of sadness threatened to ruin her good mood, but she shrugged it off.

Not today. Today, she was taking a ride with her boyfriend to visit someone.

Could she call him her boyfriend? She wasn't sure what to call what they had, but she was sure she'd know soon. One last obligation and she'd be free to live her life without a prophecy calling the shots.

Hopefully.

A knock on the door broke into her circular thoughts. She took one last look around. Once satisfied she hadn't left anything behind, she opened the door to a freshly showered Omar. He held up a single desert rose with a shy smile. When she accepted it, he gestured to her bag.

"Hi. May I take that for you?"

She passed the backpack over with a bemused smile. "Thank you. That's very kind. And thanks for the flower, I wasn't expecting..."

He shook his head. "It's nothing. I saw it outside and wanted to give you something to show you how wonderful last night was for me. I hope after today you'll still want to spend time with me."

Zahara frowned. "Of course I'll want to spend time with you. Now I'm even more nervous about this trip. Is there something I'm not going to like?"

Omar seemed to struggle meeting her eyes before finally sighing. "Honestly, I don't know. Robin was secretive about where we are going. He wouldn't even tell me the name of the person we're going to see. Just their address." He held up his phone, marked with a question mark at the destination before putting it away. "It's only an hour away from here, so we have time to get breakfast if you'd like."

Zahara shook her head. "Let's get something to eat in the car. I want to get this over with, even more so now you've made me nervous."

Omar agreed. "Sure. The sooner the better. That way, we can plan something else for the rest of our lives...er, day."

Zahara burst out laughing as his sun-darkened cheeks reddened.

Hmm, Freudian slip?

Choosing to let the comment slide, she gestured to the long hallway. "Lead on, Macduff!"

They stopped once to fill up the Jeep with petrol and grab a few snacks then headed back up the King's Highway to Shobak. Zahara enjoyed the scenery even though it was cool, just above zero Celsius. She was grateful once again for her warm sweater and coat. Her hair was completely covered with a scarf, and she found the longer she was in Jordan the more comfortable she was becoming wearing one. Maybe if she stayed she'd continue to wear it.

As they approached Shobak, the area became more agricultural with fruit and olive trees visible from the road in rows. Behind them, rising on a hill like a sentinel, was an old castle.

Noticing Zahara's interest, Omar gestured to the ancient edifice. "Shobak is one of the notable areas from the crusades. That is Montreal, which was built in 1115. It was annexed by Saladin in 1187, falling to the Ayyubid dynasty."

Her eyes widened, impressed by his knowledge. "It's beautiful. I imagine it would have been even more impressive when it wasn't a ruin."

"Likely." He laughed. "The place we are going is just a few minutes beyond here. Robin gave me that as a landmark to watch for, and I may have done a little reading around it. Mostly to get you to look at me that way." Omar winked.

She rolled her eyes at his teasing and snorted. "Of course."

But her laughter faded as they pulled down a dirt road off the main highway. She tried to take a few deep breaths to calm her racing heart, but it didn't help. She could sense Omar becoming more tense beside her, which only made her anxiety grow thinking about what lay ahead.

As they bumped down the road, she realized they were entering an orchard. It was winter so the trees were barren, but the rows were neat and well-kept, with a small skiff of snow caught in clumps of grass along the edges of hollows. The road wound around before ending at a small brown house similar to others they'd passed along the way.

Maybe we're at the wrong place. Surely, it would stand out in some way if this was where Robin wanted us to go?

When Omar pulled over and killed the engine, the vague hope disappeared. He gave her nervous smile. "Ready?"

She looked at the house again. It was simple and calm. *There's nothing to fear. There's nothing to fear.*

She lifted her chin. "As ready as I'll ever be. Surely it can't be worse than Abbas. Let's see what mystery Robin waited to spring on us until after my friends left."

Omar nodded and opened his door. Before he could come around to help her, she was out, but she did allow him to hold her hand as they walked to the door. The warmth of his skin steadied her, restoring some of the confidence she'd been pretending to have. He let go when they got to the steps, gesturing for her to go first.

Taking a deep breath, she knocked three times.

The sound echoed through the house and she took a step back. A simple knock shouldn't create so much noise. As she stepped back, the door swung open.

No one was there.

Omar peered inside, wrinkling his nose as he looked back at her. "Umm, I think that means we can enter."

Not knowing what to say, Zahara acted. Stepping into the house, she reminded herself Robin had never sent her into danger in the past and wasn't likely to start now. Taking a few more deep breaths in a futile attempt to calm down, she looked around.

They had entered a deceptively large foyer, which looked far bigger than the outside of the house. Zahara realized the house had either been magically altered to be larger inside or to look smaller outside to hide its true nature. Absolutely no way were they inside a simple cottage. The foyer was a masterpiece of marble floors and intricate Arabic lettering around the lintels on not one, but two fireplaces.

She glanced at Omar, catching his similarly stunned expression and instantly felt better. Somehow knowing he'd been caught by surprise as well made her feel less confused. She took a few more steps into the house, but there were still no signs of life. "This is creepy," she whispered.

Omar nodded, then pointed to the right. "Let's go that way."

Zahara squinted then shrugged and went toward the hall he'd suggested.

"Hello?" Her voice sounded younger to her own ears. She suspected it was because of her uncertainty, and the feeling she had they were breaking and entering.

The house remained quiet and other than appearing more castle-like as they walked, it felt empty and bare. They entered a large rectangular room with a wood table at least twenty feet long surrounded by tapestries on the walls. It was elegant and formal, but oddly cozy somehow.

"What is this place?" Omar looked around with disbelief. "Robin didn't say anything about this."

Zahara spotted a light glowing at the other end of the banquet room and elbowed him. "There, do you see that? Quickly!"

She picked up the pace until she was almost jogging, Omar's footsteps just behind her. She didn't look away from the light as it moved away faster. Something told her this was what they'd been looking for and she didn't want to lose sight of it.

They followed it through several twists and turns, never losing it but also never catching sight of who or what they were following. Suddenly they entered a room with a large bay of windows that looked like a flower shop.

Zahara skidded to a stop and Omar bumped into her before catching himself. She stared at the room. Trees and flowers covered every available surface and the air was fragrant. A few chairs and benches broke up the greenery and she realized they were in a solarium. Her heart welled with joy at the lush nature around her.

It was an earth mage's paradise.

It took some time before she could draw her attention away. She still didn't know who or what they'd chased into the room and she rescanned the room for the light now. Then she saw it—a white glow tucked behind one of the larger trees.

She crept toward it, trying to step as silently as possible to keep the light from running away again. But this time, the light stayed put and she rounded the tree to find a small bed.

Lying motionless in the center, surrounded by plants and flowers, was an old woman.

CHAPTER 26

Zahara stepped forward, then stopped, unsure what to do. She looked at Omar, bracing herself when he waved her forward.

"Hello?" Her voice cracked and the woman didn't stir, so she repeated herself louder. "Hello?"

She was so still Zahara initially thought she was a statue. So when the woman's eyes snapped open, Zahara jumped back in surprise. She looked at Zahara, scanning her from the top of her bright green scarf to her puffy jacket and her jeans, then a smile crept over her face.

"At long last, you've come back."

The voice was as creaky as a door that hadn't been oiled in years but sounded oddly familiar.

Where have I heard it before?

She racked her brain, drawing her eyebrows together as she concentrated. The woman noticed and began to laugh.

"Oh, Zahara. Has it truly been that long? So long you don't remember?"

She sat up carefully in bed, moving her joints in a way that suggested she was stiff and sore, and when she finally stood, she wobbled a little before grabbing an intricate wood staff for support.

Neither Zahara nor Omar moved as she stomped toward them with a smiling face and inclined her head to the side, waving her free hand toward the solarium.

"Come, let us sit together in the drawing room. It has been awhile since I last had company, and I wish to have a proper tea."

Zahara stepped back to let the woman pass, and when she looked at the solarium, her mouth dropped open. She'd noticed the chairs and benches when they'd walked through earlier, but the room had changed in the minute since she'd seen it. Now a table with a steaming tea pot and plates of snacks waited for them.

Zahara whirled around, but no one else was there. "How?"

She hadn't realized she'd asked the question aloud until the woman smiled.

"Well, magic of course!"

She'd arranged herself on a cushioned chair with an ottoman stool, propping her feet up, and waited until Zahara and Omar sat at the table before speaking again.

"Please, help yourself to tea and biscuits. I don't get much in the way of company these days, but I'm even happier to see you here in particular, Zahara."

"How do you know my name? I'm sorry, but I don't know you. Should I?" She hoped she wasn't being horribly rude. As sweet as the old woman seemed, Zahara truly had no idea who she was.

"Has it been so long?" The woman sighed, looking down at her hands with a wistfulness which struck Zahara to the heart. "I'm not the woman I was, once upon a time, so maybe it's fair you don't recognize me." She looked at Zahara, tilting her head as their eyes met. "Together, we created something magical. The amulet you are wearing."

Zahara looked down. The necklace had begun to glow a faint green in response to the woman's words and her eyes went wide.

"It can't be. Reema?"

The woman smiled and as she did, Zahara saw a faint echo of the young woman she'd known, shining through the wrinkles of the older one before her.

"Yes, Zahara, it is."

"But how? That was centuries ago!"

Reema nodded. "It was. But that night changed many things for me, altering my human destiny. After you left, Abbas flew into a rage. If he hadn't been in such a hurry to catch you, I'm sure he would have made sure we were actually dead. But he merely used his magic to throw me against the wall of the tent before leaving to go after you, forgetting all about us in his fury."

Zahara blinked rapidly against the tears threatening to blind her. "It was the hardest thing I ever did, leaving you there. I wanted to stay and fight, to protect Haytham, but the amulet..."

Reema shook her head. "Shush, child. I told you to go. We both know you had to get the amulet to the portal. He would have won and we all would have died if you hadn't succeeded. Clearly, you did, although at the time I had no way to know what happened other than that he left and didn't return."

She sighed, shaking her head as her hands plucked at her dress, pale and thin. She looked at them briefly before staring out of the nearby window.

"We left too, of course. After everything that happened, I couldn't stay there any longer. Haytham had a broken arm from being thrown in his hawk form but was otherwise uninjured. I suffered from headaches for a long while but was able to function well enough to care for him until he returned to health."

Zahara watched Reema's eyes fill with tears as her voice broke with the memory.

"Before we left, I buried my *Umi* with my memory of Marwan. It took time, and I worried Abbas would return before I was done, but I couldn't leave without showing my love and respect. I dug a beautiful grave, praying I would someday see them again."

Zahara felt the hot wetness of tears on her cheeks and quickly wiped them away. "I'm so sorry I couldn't save them."

Reema smiled, her eyes brightening. "It was our destiny. You were never meant to save them, only to ensure Haytham and the amulet made it. After you left, a visitor came and explained the prophecy, cautioning me to keep it to myself until some point in the future, when he would send you back to hear the rest of the story."

Zahara leaned forward, cocking her head. "Robin?"

Reema nodded. "Yes, it was Robin who came. He told me he was out of his realm, but as this was an important matter relating to earth and magic, he could promise me that someday, a resolution would arrive."

Zahara shook her head. "How did he know? The prophecy was long before I was born. He explained Abbas had it only partially correct, but not how he found out in the first place."

Reema chuckled weakly. "Who's to say with the ancient ones? It's a common problem with prophecies, you know. Men always believe they know the truth of a matter when in reality, prophecies are slippery things, created by gods and magic. As lesser beings, we almost never discover the whole truth."

It was Omar's turn to lean in. "Did he tell you when the prophecy came about and how?"

"Well," she began. "Not exactly. He told me the prophecy about Marwan's descendant controlling earth magic for the area we now call the Middle East. Abbas, as we know, assumed that meant a son, which wasn't an unusual assumption to make, especially during that time.

Reema took a sip of her tea and frustration began to bubble inside Zahara.

Reema is nearly as bad as Robin at drawing things out.

She took a deep breath and shoved the impatience down, knowing the story was old and likely difficult for the other woman to share.

"But as you know, the wording of prophecies is a tricky thing. It never meant son, but descendant, which was you all along. Robin shared the information with me back then, and helped protect our family all this time. When we migrated over generations, first to Pakistan and then further, to the British Isles, he kept watch. Did you ever wonder why a god of the earth would spend so much time playing with a child?"

Zahara had never really thought of it before this journey, but looking back now she understood how unusual her childhood had been. She'd always had her Robin whenever she'd needed him. When she compared that to Cat's ongoing and frequently voiced frustration about how absent Robin was whenever she had questions, it was easy to see she'd been a special case all along.

"Why me? What made me so unique?"

It was a question she'd been asking herself since her mum had called her home to give her the necklace, one Robin had glossed over when she'd tried to ask him.

Reema shrugged. "Why not you? You were born with a stubborn streak a mile wide and three brothers to help you grow strong. You are quick-witted with earth magic to spare. I mailed the amulet to you because I knew it was meant for only you to wield."

Zahara's jaw dropped. "You mailed it? Wait— *you're* the Aunt Reema my mum said died? I thought I understood but now I'm confused again."

She looked at Omar's blank face, feeling better he hadn't seen that revelation coming either.

"I'm not dead yet, but I'm not far from that long-awaited moment." She gestured to herself with a shaky hand. "Robin came to me again a few weeks ago. He said everything was aligned and it was finally time to activate the prophecy."

She held out her hands for Zahara. When she took them, she felt how frail Reema was as her hands trembled slightly in her younger grip.

"I had no idea if or how you would succeed, but I knew the fate of our family rested in very capable hands. Because of you, Haytham was able to grow to a strong and wonderful man, who gave me many beautiful grand-babies and great-grandbabies." Reema smiled as a tear slipped down her cheek. "I was blessed and cursed to watch it all."

Zahara shook her head, horrified as Reema voiced something she'd wondered. "How have you lived so long?"

Reema shrugged. "I'm sure it was the amulet. Once you left my time, the amulet split. Part of it stayed behind in that cave where I found it the next day while looking for you. I kept it safe until it was time to mail it to you. By casting the spell, you activated it, making it whole again."

Zahara shook her head. "I remember Marwan saying the amulet was of all times and places. So strange."

"Yes. I believe the power within the amulet kept me young long after I should have died and become part of the desert sand. Now that it is out of my keeping and in yours at last, I feel my time growing short. I shall soon pass into the wind and join my dearest loved ones."

Zahara jerked her hand back, covering her mouth to hold back a sob. "How did you ever manage to live with such loss?"

Reema shook her head. "I always knew it was temporary. Time is fleeting, but love is forever. I had the hope once I returned the amulet to its rightful owner, I would finally be able to join my loved ones. I am grateful you have arrived at long last, and thank you for succeeding. Most of all, thank you for accepting your destiny, as difficult as it has been."

Zahara tilted her head up, taking a deep breath to hold back her emotions. This was about the other woman. Her tears were not important in comparison to what she had survived.

"I am so sorry, Reema. I had no idea your life had been so difficult."

Reema's face glowed with happiness, but Zahara noticed she'd developed more wrinkles in the time they'd been speaking.

"No, Zahara, it wasn't difficult. It was amazing. I had a chance to live hundreds of years with the memory of my loved ones and the knowledge you would arrive when the fates aligned. It is easy to hold onto hope when there is no doubt. I knew you would come because you already had."

Zahara pressed her lips together, knowing she truly meant it.

When Reema looked at Omar then back to Zahara, her smile faded. "One last thing I must inform you of may be more difficult, but I want you to understand the entire tale."

"There's more?" Zahara couldn't think what else Reema could say to top everything else she'd shared.

"Abbas had a daughter."

Zahara blinked, underwhelmed. "Oh yeah. I forgot. What happened to her?"

Reema smiled, looking off into the distance. "She was a nice girl. I met her once in passing and felt horrible. I had, after all, stolen away the man she'd been promised to marry. But she was a sweet and loving soul, nothing like her father except for her magic. Her mother had been a local Bedouin, with her own desert magic which gave her another, truer form she preferred after leaving court."

Omar's voice was hesitant, almost fearful. "She could shift into a fox, couldn't she?"

Reema rewarded him with a smile. "She could. A red fox, in fact."

Suddenly, the pieces came together. The red fox who'd helped her during her flight from Abbas in the desert. She'd assumed the fox was male, and a natural fox at that. Had it been Abbas's own daughter all along?

"Was she the one I saw? And if so, why would she help me against her own father?"

"Because she wasn't evil. She could recognize love when she saw it and had never been keen to marry a man who didn't love her in return. The last I heard was once the wedding had been called off, she returned to her mother's people in the desert. I assumed she'd hidden away somewhere far from her father to raise children of her own. Once Robin filled in the blanks, I had even more reason to be grateful to her."

Reema looked at Omar, raising an eyebrow. "But I think you may already have suspected this part of the story; didn't you, Omar?"

Zahara turned, feeling unexpectedly betrayed. Her thoughts must have shown on her face, because Omar looked down at his hands before firming his mouth and meeting her eyes.

"I didn't know how to tell you. My family has been in the area for a long, long time, which you already knew. How was I supposed to tell you I thought I was a descendant of the same jinn who tried to kill your family? The reason you were here in my homeland to begin with? Robin asked me to help you, but once I met you, I just couldn't tell you. At first, I didn't know it was important, and by the time I did, I was certain it would drive you away. I discovered...I needed you in my life."

Zahara blinked, letting everything sink in as the hurt settled. Reema was still alive, the red fox who'd helped her had been the daughter of Abbas, and Omar was descended from her. If that wasn't a prophecy, she didn't know what the hell else was. Finally, at the desperation she recognized in his eyes, she relented.

"Um, wow. That's pretty complicated."

When he looked as if he would crumple, she burst into laughter at the bizarreness of the situation. How could she be mad at him when a prophecy was clearly beyond his control?

"It's okay, Omar. I won't hold you responsible for this as long as you don't blame me for my part in the family feud we inadvertently share."

Omar sighed. "Oh, praise Allah. I was positive you wouldn't want me in your life once you knew the truth. I couldn't blame you if you didn't speak to me ever again."

"Why would I blame you for your ancestors? I wouldn't have escaped Abbas if it hadn't been for the one who helped me. You are as much her descendant as you are his."

Tension drained from his face and he held out one tentative hand. When she took it, his smile spread from ear to ear.

"As long as you aren't angry with me, I'll take whatever reasoning works for you. I promise never to lie, even by omission, from now on."

Reema's weak voice broke into their reconciliation and Zahara realized she'd almost forgotten the other woman in her attempt to reassure Omar. When she turned back to her, she gasped when she saw the woman had aged at least twenty years.

"Reema! What's wrong?"

She smiled, coughing weakly. "My time is drawing near. Can you take me back to bed? I'd like to go surrounded by plants with the window open. The sun feels so nice against my face."

Zahara and Omar leapt to their feet, supporting, almost carrying Reema to her bed by the end of the short walk. Zahara tucked her in with quilts, watching as her skin sank against her bones.

When she was settled into bed, Reema opened her eyes and smiled with joy. "I'm going to be with my love. I wish you both the happiness I had with my Marwan but many more years to enjoy together, watching your own children and grandchildren grow in the light. May Allah bless you and keep you safe."

With those words, Reema closed her eyes for the last time.

Her skin became translucent and began to glow faintly. Zahara blinked away tears as Reema vanished into specks of light which floated toward the window, becoming part of the sunshine streaming down onto the bed.

For the second time since everything had conspired to pull Zahara out of her routine, she broke down and sobbed. With her hands covering her face, she cried for Reema and her long life alone without Marwan, for the woman who'd had to watch her precious son grow up and have children, then watch all of them die from the ravages of age and life. She wouldn't have been strong enough to bear everything Reema had.

Omar reached out to put his arm around her shoulder. Even in her grief she felt his uncertainty. She knew he still wasn't sure if he was welcome in her life. At that moment, fixing that suddenly seemed to be the most important thing in the world.

Flinging herself into his arms, she sobbed with everything she'd kept bottled up. The sorrow of watching people die, her terror and pain, the triumph, and even the love. She'd never felt so many emotions in such a short period of time.

Slowly, the storm of feelings began to abate and she became aware of her surroundings again. She was in Reema's castle, in the warm circle of Omar's arms. Her tears faded into the dull headache she always acquired from crying as she gave him a watery smile, then winked at his concerned expression.

"Well, this was quite the family reunion. Anything else you or Robin want to share? I'm not sure how many more surprises I can handle, but I'd like the truth now, while everything's fresh."

"I think that's it. You know about my deep, dark family secret now. It's the only thing I've been hiding. As for Robin, I'm never sure what he's going to pull next so I can't be held responsible for him. This was the last thing he asked of me, but he also said if you liked it here, the house was yours. Apparently, he has another secret gate to Summerland located in the orchard outside."

Zahara suddenly realized during the entire time she'd been away, she'd never even thought to let her family know what had been happening. "Oh my goodness, my parents! They must be so worried."

Omar shook his head. "Evelyn let them know what was happening. You were understandably busy and she didn't want them to worry."

Zahara let out a sigh. "Well, that's good. I guess I should let them know I'm not coming home anytime soon. My mum will be devastated. As wonderful as they are, I doubt they'll be happy to find out I'll be living so far away."

He let go of her hand and walked toward the window, staring out at the trees for a minute before turning back with hope shining in his eyes.

"It's a little sudden, but I'd love for you to introduce me to your parents."

Zahara had followed him to the window and stared at him now. His gaze darted away, looking everywhere but directly at her. What he was really asking was clear.

"Listen, Omar. I'm fine if you want to meet them, but I'm a modern girl. You're going to need to spend some time impressing me first if you want to even consider getting serious." She gave him a mock-stern glare. "After all, my destiny clearly hinges on my stubborn streak. I'll only settle for love."

A smile crept over Omar's face. "I think I can handle your terms. Let's call your parents and tell them where you are."

Zahara smiled and walked into his arms. The sun spilled through the window onto the indoor jungle, bathing them in light as he lifted her up and spun her around.

CHAPTER 27

Zahara smiled as Omar played with their youngest. Every time she saw him with their children, her love for him multiplied. The last five years had been amazing, give or take the usual good-vs-evil stuff they'd had to handle.

Once she'd spoken with her mum and told her what had happened, both of her parents had been at her new house within the week to meet Omar. To her great relief, they'd hit it off immediately. Things with Omar had progressed naturally from then to the point where Zahara had been happy to receive a proposal blessed by both of her parents. In fact, Zahara was suspicious her parents visited as often as they did now to see him instead of her, but she didn't mind in the slightest.

The house, which she still thought of as Reema's, was amazing. It had become a wonderful family home. While it remained deceptively small from the outside, it possessed more than enough room to fit everyone in their family. Luckily, Omar's family preferred a more nomadic lifestyle and were infrequent visitors, and Zahara's parents still had the farm and her brothers to worry about marrying off, so they were only occasionally there.

They'd married within a year of the prophecy being complete, and their first son arrived a year after that, followed a year later by a daughter every bit as stubborn as Zahara. A fact which her mum gleefully pointed out when the infant Reema refused to eat any solids unless she could do it herself.

Zahara loved her children and husband more than anything and thought often of Reema, wishing she'd been able to spend more time with her. She'd been an amazing woman and lived an incredible life.

Zahara looked at the amulet she rarely took off and smiled at its comforting green glow. The magic was hers to guard and with Omar's help, they did a good job. The land was prosperous and peaceful in a way it hadn't been for centuries.

Just then, he turned and caught her watching them. He blew her a kiss and she smiled, absently touching her stomach. When he saw the reflexive movement, his eyes widened and she laughed, knowing love was always better when there was more of it to share.

Don't miss out!

Visit the website below and you can sign up to receive emails whenever H. M. Gooden publishes a new book. There's no charge and no obligation.

https://books2read.com/r/B-A-POWE-BGVZ

BOOKS 2 READ

Connecting independent readers to independent writers.

Did you love *Zahara's Quest*? Then you should read *The Phoenix and the Witch*[1] by H. M. Gooden!

Fresh from their triumph against Dub in San Francisco, the girls are content to return to their normal lives, unaware that their fight against the darkness is not over.

Although they succeeded in destroying their previous adversaries, another threat has risen in a far away country.

This time, they must travel to Edinburgh to confront the darkest of all evils.

The origin.

---

1. https://books2read.com/u/bxqWgJ

2. https://books2read.com/u/bxqWgJ

Will they succeed in fighting back the dark or will they be left irrevocably changed?

As the conclusion to the original trilogy, this adventure will set the course for everything in their lives and they will learn that even their friends may not be entirely what they seem.

Read more at https://www.hmgoodenauthor.com/.

Also by H. M. Gooden

The Dragons of the North
Mai's First Date

The Raven and the Witch Hunter
The Raven and the Witch Hunter: The Spirit of Big Bear
The Raven and the Witch Hunter: The Wedding
The Raven and The Witch Hunter: Honeymoon and Full
Moon Blues
Wendigo

The Rise of the Light
Fiona's Gift
Dream of Darkness
The Stone Dragon
The Phoenix and the Witch
Dragons are Forever
The Raven and the Witch Hunter
Zahara's Quest

Standalone
The Raven and the Witch Hunter Omnibus: Volumes 2-4
To Capture the Heart of Spring
Darkness on the Nile
I was a Teenage Vegetarian Zombie Detective

Watch for more at https://www.hmgoodenauthor.com/.

About the Author

H. M. Gooden has always loved the world of books, but over the last few years a new story has begged to be told, and as a result, this series was born.

In between dealing with children and work, the majority of the actual writing happens between four and six am and involves multiple cups of coffee for inspiration.

You can always find me on Twitter, Facebook, Instagram, Bookbub and Goodreads.

I always love to hear from readers!

Read more at https://www.hmgoodenauthor.com/.